"Mr. Tl

Grant raised his head from his paperwork and saw the face of a dead woman. Helen Fremont.

He dropped his pen, stiffened his back and stared.

It was her—exactly. Long blond hair, even features, crystalline blue eyes. Had they made a mistake? Had she managed to ski to safety?

The prickles, which had danced along the skin on his hands and neck, subsided. Not a ghost after all; this had to be Helen's sister, whom he'd contacted in Toronto a little while ago and informed of the tragedy.

"We were identical twins," Amalie Fremont said. "I take it you didn't know. You didn't like her very much, did you?" she added.

That was an understatement. He'd first met the woman shortly before Christmas, and found her flighty, brittle and insincere. He liked her even less now. Undoubtedly, her reckless skiing had caused the avalanche, and his best friend was dead because of her.

If only she'd never passed through their quiet mountain community. Her brand of trouble belonged in the big city as far as he was concerned. As for her twin sister, he was less sure. Amalie Fremont's gaze held qualities of intelligence and reserve that he'd never glimpsed in Helen.

Plus there was that inexplicable buzz he'd felt from just shaking her hand....

Dear Reader,

I've often made the drive from Calgary to Vancouver through the Rocky Mountains. One year I was with my husband and two daughters, when we decided to stop at the information center at Rogers Pass. That was where I first saw the video *Snow Wars*, and decided that a man who worked at Avalanche Control would make a perfect hero for a romance novel.

Several years passed before I developed the plot to suit my hero and had my editor's approval to go ahead with the book. Now I needed to drive back to Rogers Pass to flesh out the details for my story.

I have to be honest. Some books are just more fun to research than others. The men at Avalanche Control in Rogers Pass couldn't have been more helpful. Together we worked through different scenes in my book, melding my storytelling ideas with the physical realities of the setting. They shared tales of successful rescues and of heartbreaking tragedies. Cheerfully, they endured all my questions, from "How long do the batteries in an avalanche transceiver last?" to "How many minutes can someone survive once buried by an avalanche?"

I hope that in this book I've done justice to their answers and their profession.

Readers, I'd love to hear from you. You can e-mail me at cjcarmichael@SuperAuthors.com. Or write to Suite #1754— 246 Stewart Green S.W., Calgary, Alberta, T3H 3C8 Canada.

Sincerely,

C.J. *Carmichael*

A Sister Would Know
C.J. Carmichael

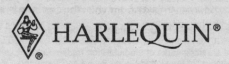

HARLEQUIN®

TORONTO • NEW YORK • LONDON
AMSTERDAM • PARIS • SYDNEY • HAMBURG
STOCKHOLM • ATHENS • TOKYO • MILAN • MADRID
PRAGUE • WARSAW • BUDAPEST • AUCKLAND

ISBN 0-373-70968-4

A SISTER WOULD KNOW

Visit us at www.eHarlequin.com

Printed in U.S.A.

For my sisters, Kathy and Patti, with love

ACKNOWLEDGMENTS

Thanks to those real-life heroes in Rogers Pass
for their generous assistance with my research:
Dave Skjonsberg, manager, Avalanche Control;
Jeff Goodrich and John Kelly, avalanche observers;
Alan Polster, park warden, Glacier National Park.

Thanks, also, to Pat Dunn, at Parks Canada,
who helped me gather much useful material.

Any factual errors are mine.

PROLOGUE

HELENA FREMONT KNEW that her dilemma was at last resolved. Her obligations to Davin, her baby, had been taken out of her hands.

Panic choked a cry from her throat. She couldn't move; she couldn't see. Burning pain shot up from her left leg—broken—but this was the least of her problems.

Air. How much had been buried with her? How long would it last?

The avalanche had carried her too far, buried her too deep to hope for rescue. When the oxygen that had been submerged with her was gone, she would soon follow.

I'm sorry, baby. Please forgive me.

The noon sun had been shining through the light curtain of falling snowflakes an hour earlier when she and Ramsey had set out for their day of skiing. Now, in her coffin of packed powder, Helena held the picture of her infant boy in her mind. She saw him as he'd been in the minutes after his extraction from her womb, over eleven years ago. The last time she'd set eyes on him.

That labor, the birth, her experiences after... Even now, her final minutes ticking away, the memory was a horror. Better to go like this—a slow, but relatively painless death.

Better for her, perhaps... Guilt pressed in like the snow above her head. Fifteen minutes ago she'd laughed at the risk of an avalanche. Her companion, Ramsey Carter, had tried to steer her along the safe ridge that he'd mapped out in the small wooden shack where they'd spent the night.

But the virgin drifts on the sloping bowl had been too inviting. She'd dug in her poles and pointed her ski tips toward the inviting concave mountain basin. Around her the snow lay in thick scallops from the previous day's storm. The whoosh and scratch of her skis against the ice crystals were the only sounds as she swooped down the 35° slope.

Except for Ramsey's cry. "Helen!"

She'd laughed and tucked her body lower to the ground. Funny how many ways there were to outrun pain. She never would've guessed skiing on the edge of her control could be one of them. She almost felt she was flying. Then suddenly she really was in the air. She glanced down and couldn't see her feet.

Something hit her from behind and she was falling, ski poles dangling wildly from the safety straps attached to her wrists.

Now the snow was no longer fluffy, but hard,

concrete stuff that burned her skin and bruised her bones as she was sucked deeper within it. The skis, which had allowed her to skim the crystal surface just minutes before, were now anchors dragging her down. Her flailing arms became imprisoned in the mounting piles of snow, ensnared, too, by their attached poles.

When her free fall finally stopped, she was like a butterfly mounted on Styrofoam. Movement was impossible. How much snow settled above her? She had no idea. All she knew was that she was packed in and everything around her was dark and absolutely still.

In the isolating darkness, it was a shock to realize she could still hear the world above—tree limbs rubbing in the stiff breeze, the squawking from a couple of disturbed whiskey jacks. She tried to struggle, but her range of motion was limited to the wriggling of her fingers from hands spread out sideways to her body.

Too late she wished she had kept them in front of her face before she was buried. Snow pressed in on her eyes, against her nose and mouth, making it a struggle to gasp for air.

Had Ramsey seen the avalanche in time? Been able to ski to safety? She hoped he hadn't followed her, wasn't at this moment risking his life for hers.

Flashes of light played before her eyes. She knew the snow must be cold, but her body beneath the tight ski pants and Nordic sweater felt warm, the pain in her leg almost trifling. She listened for Ramsey's voice above, but moments passed and she heard nothing.

She hoped he would be safe. It was only fair. He, after all, had a family to return to. While she did not.

She thought of Davin, her baby, her love. Poor baby. Regret pounded through her veins, along with her cooling blood. What was she doing here? She never should have left the first time. Nor the second…

Desperate for air, she opened her mouth and took in dry granules of snow, instead. Realizing her mistake, she tried to spit them out, but her face was packed in too tightly. Panic built, then exploded. From low in her chest she let out a scream that no one would hear.

The scream went on and on, until her lungs were burning and the ringing drove all other sound from her ears.

Inside her head, her scream had a name, and her mind conjured a face identical to the one she saw reflected in the mirror every morning. Her last conscious thought was a plea for help.

Amalie! I can't breathe! Help me, Amalie!

CHAPTER ONE

IT WAS JANUARY, and cold to be standing outside in the snow, but eleven-year-old Davin Fremont didn't mind. He laughed as his aunt Amalie took a wild swing at the piñata strung up in his best friend's backyard—and missed.

"Come on, guys," his aunt pleaded, her eyes covered by a tightly knotted scarf. "Give me a clue. Right or left?"

"Left!" one of the kids at the party yelled.

"Right!" shot back Jeremy, the birthday boy.

Amalie stumbled in the snow, unaware that the papier-mâché sheriff hung precisely over her head. A gust of wind set it spinning and Davin yearned for the candies and trading cards he knew were stuffed into the hollow form.

"No clues," he said, hoping he'd get another turn with the bat. "It isn't fair."

"Oh, sure. Fair. I didn't hear any talk about fairness when *you* were up here, Davin."

"Maybe we should give her another spin." Jeremy's mother was laughing almost as hard as Davin. When a couple of the boys started to run toward Amalie, she leaped forward to restrain them. "I was only kidding! She's having a hard enough time as it is."

"Just wait until it's your turn, Jen," Amalie threatened.

"No doubt you'll have the piñata shattered before then."

"Jenny, if I had any idea where you were standing, I just might be tempted..." His aunt raised the plastic baseball bat in her hands threateningly.

Davin saw Jeremy smirk and he laughed, too. It was fun the way his aunt and Mrs. Mitchell teased each other. They'd been friends a long time. Gone to university together, and now worked at the same hospital. Davin and Jeremy were going to do the same thing when they grew up.

"Come on, swing the bat!" urged one impatient party guest.

That was when Davin noticed his aunt wasn't moving. It was like she'd frozen solid. A second later she moaned and collapsed to her knees.

"Aunty?" He glanced at Jeremy's mom and dad. The concern on their faces made him scared. He ran for his aunt and threw both arms around her, as Jeremy's dad whisked the scarf off her face.

Aunt Amalie didn't seem to notice. She was bending over her stomach, her mouth open. "I ca-can't breathe!"

Davin hugged tighter, more afraid than he'd ever been in his life. Was his aunt dying?

"Honey, give her some space." He felt Mrs. Mitchell pry his arms away. His aunt was on the ground now, curled into a ball, her hands at her throat.

"Stand back, boys! Should I call 911?" Mr. Mitchell sounded tense.

"I'm not sure. It's almost like an epileptic fit, but Amalie isn't—" Crouched in the snow next to his aunt, Jennifer was holding Davin with one hand while she observed her friend. "She *is* breathing, though she seems to be having trouble drawing in air. Amalie, can you hear me? Is your chest hurting?"

"Yes. No. It's my leg..." Suddenly, his aunt went still again. "I can't move!"

What in the world was happening? Davin began to whimper; he was so scared....

He felt the cold bite of the winter wind as Jennifer withdrew her arm from his shoulder. As he watched, she reached for his now-motionless aunt. Gently she picked up her wrist with one hand, brushing snow from her face with the other.

"Amalie, it's okay."

His aunt blinked.

Davin rushed forward again, this time just taking her hand, the one Mrs. Mitchell wasn't holding.

His aunt's gaze shifted to him. She blinked, then

gave a wobbly smile. "I guess I missed the piñata, huh?"

Relief was sweeter than the icing on Jeremy's birthday cake. "You're all right?"

"Of course I am, buddy." But she looked shaky as Mrs. Mitchell helped her sit up from the snow.

"Amalie? What happened?"

"I'm not sure, Jen. It was really weird. But I'm okay. I promise."

Jeremy glanced at Mr. Mitchell's face. He seemed relieved. Mrs. Mitchell, too, was smiling. He scrambled to his feet and held out his hands to help his aunt stand. If all the adults thought this was okay, then it must be.

"I'm sorry to break up the party, Jen, but I think we'd better leave."

Mrs. Mitchell gave her a hug. "Let Aaron drive you home."

"Really, I'm fine." Her smile was as bright as ever, and now that she was standing, she was steady and strong.

They were in the car, when Mrs. Mitchell suddenly remembered the treat bags and had Jeremy run to the house to get Davin's.

"Thanks for inviting me to your party," Davin said, accepting the bright blue-and-yellow bag through the open passenger window.

"Take care, now!" Everyone waved as his aunt pulled the car out onto the street.

It was cold in the car and quiet. Davin peered at the treat bag in his lap but didn't feel like checking to see what was inside.

Instead, he checked his aunt. She looked normal, except her skin was kind of white and she was driving slower than usual.

At the next red light, she gave him a smile. "I'm okay. Really, Davin."

"Then why—"

Her gloved hand reached for his shoulder. "Do you remember my telling you that when Helena is hurt I always know because I get the same feeling?"

Oh-oh. He should have figured this was all connected to Amalie's twin. Everything bad in his life somehow tied in with her. The mother he wished he didn't have.

Davin shut his mouth and didn't ask any more questions.

AMALIE NOTICED Davin's withdrawal, so common whenever the subject of Helena came up. When the traffic light turned green again, she took her hand from his shoulder and placed it back on the steering wheel.

She felt badly that she'd spoiled the end of the party for him. And just when they were having so much fun. But the urge to rush home was some thing she couldn't ignore...maybe she'd find some word from Helena.

She and Davin lived in a rented duplex about six blocks from the Mitchells in Bloor West Village. The Toronto neighborhood was handy to the hospital Amalie worked at—she could take the subway with just one transfer. The neighborhood had once been run-down, but now it was considered trendy. Amalie appreciated the blend of new and old in the shops and cafés that lined both sides of Bloor street.

Since completing her training as a nutritionist, she had dreamed of one day buying the house she now rented. But real estate prices were sky-high for the two-story brick dwellings, with their tiny front porches and high-pitched roofs. It didn't seem to matter that the buildings were small and packed tight together, many with original plumbing and wiring.

Location, location, location. They were close to the subway, to downtown Toronto, to the lake, to just about everything, it seemed.

Amalie rolled her Jetta behind the Dodge Omni that belonged to the neighbors who lived in the other half of her duplex, then turned to her nephew buckled into the front seat beside her.

"I'm sorry if I scared you, Davin."

He hadn't uttered a word since she'd made that reference to her sister. Amalie put her hand to Davin's head and brushed back hair so fair it was practically white. His eyes shone like clear blue topaz, in the dwindling afternoon light. With coloring just like hers, and her sister's, Davin had been an exceptionally beautiful child.

But that was changing. Just this year his features had begun to lose their little-boy roundness, taking on a definite masculine shape. He was growing up. Inside, however, he was still her little boy. Too young to understand the odd emotional connection that existed between her and her identical twin.

"Hungry?"

He shook his head.

"Well, how about a cup of hot cocoa, then?" Amalie turned off the ignition and got out of the car. As she removed the glove from her right hand so she could search for the house keys in her purse, she felt the bite of the northwesterly wind on her cheeks and her hand. It was almost February, and while the days had begun to lengthen, the recent interval of cold weather was a reminder that spring was still a good two months away.

Warm air and the lingering aroma from the cinnamon French toast she'd made for breakfast welcomed her as she opened the front door. Letting her nephew go ahead, Amalie stomped the snow from her boots, watching it scatter over the gray-painted boards of the porch floor.

Once inside she passed along the narrow hallway to the kitchen at the back of the house. Immedi ately, she scanned the kitchen counter. Sure enough, the red light on the answering machine was flashing.

Davin had disappeared into the living room. She could hear a murmur from the television, and decided against calling him back to pick up the ski jacket and mitts he'd left lying on the floor.

Looking past tired, oak-veneer cupboards, dull yellowed linoleum and cracked and chipped countertops, Amalie reached for the playback button on the machine with a shaking hand.

You have one message.

She dropped to a kitchen chair and stared out the window. A weathered maple dominated the narrow strip of yard. To her the branches appeared weary after a valiant season of struggling against freezing temperatures, driving winds and snowfall after snowfall.

The machine clicked, and her mother's recorded voice came out at her.

"Hello, Amalie. Just wondering why you hadn't phoned yet this weekend. Your father and I are fine, although Dad's back is aching after shoveling all that snow from last night's storm. I hope you and Davin managed to go to church this morning. Give us a call when you get in."

No word from Helena after all. Amalie's disappointment fused with the guilt she felt about not going home this weekend as usual and shoveling that long driveway for her father.

She knew the guilt was irrational. Jeremy's party had been important to Davin, and he deserved a little fun. Weekends with her parents in the small town north of Toronto ran a predictable pattern. Saturday, she did the odd chores they couldn't seem to manage on their own. Sunday, all four of them went to church in the morning, then came home for a big midday meal. Afterward, she and Davin piled in the car for the two-and-a-half-hour drive home.

Only occasionally did she and Davin remain in Toronto for a weekend, but when they did, her mother created such a fuss it was hardly worth it. For instance, that reminder about church. Her mother knew Jeremy's party had been scheduled for Sunday at eleven.

Her friend Jenny was always bugging her about taking too much responsibility for her parents. "You need to lighten up and have a little fun," she urged over and over again.

But Jenny had two brothers and a sister, and her mom and dad weren't the type to make demands on their children.

Amalie's family was totally different. Her parents had immigrated from Germany when she and Helena were only seven, and they'd never fully integrated into their new country. As they got older, they relied on her more and more, and she felt she owed them whatever help she could offer.

Especially since she knew that she and Helena had both been such disappointments to them.

Amalie reached for the phone, then decided not to return her mother's call at the moment, in order to keep the line open. With any luck she would hear from Helena soon, so she could stop worrying.

If only there were some way for her to contact her sister. But Helena's occasional note or gift for Davin rarely included a return address. Her phone calls were even less frequent, and Amalie had learned not to ask where she lived or what her phone number was.

The two sisters hadn't actually seen each other since Davin's birth, and he was already eleven.

Yet Amalie had never needed to see her sister to know when she was in trouble.

"Oh, Helena, where are you?" Amalie laid her head down on the kitchen table, atop her folded arms. Being an identical twin was part blessing, part burden. To be so close to another human being meant never to be truly alone. But it also meant having to struggle for a separate identity.

For Helena, that struggle had been harder. Amalie was certain that was why she'd moved so far from home, so rarely kept in touch.

It was because of her, and the knowledge hurt. Firstborn, Amalie had always felt responsible for

Helena. Yet no matter how she tried, in the end she'd always let her sister down.

Closing her eyes, she attempted to focus in on her subconscious communication with her sister. Amalie pressed her hands to her temples, tightened her jaw. *Phone me, Helena!*

But it wasn't until the following evening that the call finally came. And it wasn't from her sister.

AMALIE WAS LIFTING the lid from a pot of boiling water when she heard the first ring. The lid slipped from her fingers and fell back on the pot with a clash, sending bubbling water spraying over the element, where it hissed angrily.

She turned off the heat, then reached for the phone, praying it wouldn't be another call from her mother.

"Hello?"

A throat cleared over the line before a man identified himself. "This is Grant Thorlow. I'm the manager of the Avalanche Control Section of Highway Services in Glacier National Park."

The bombardment of words, none of them familiar, had her groping for pen and paper. First she scribbled down his name: Grant Thorlow. "Where did you say you were calling from?"

"Rogers Pass," he said. "That's in British Columbia."

"Yes. Of course." The treacherous Rocky

Mountain corridor of the Trans-Canada Highway was a well-known Canadian landmark.

"I was wondering…" He paused, and she could hear him swallow. "Is there any chance you're acquainted with a woman named Helen Fremont?"

This was it. She clung to the receiver, fear and hope making her heart pound. "Do you mean Helena?"

"I don't think so. It says Helen here on her bank card."

Amalie discounted the small difference. Helena had never been happy with the old-fashioned German names their parents had baptized them with. "What does she look like?"

The resulting pause was alarming, giving Amalie time to consider possibilities. There'd been an accident. Helena was in the hospital.

"Tall, blond, blue eyes," he said finally. "In her late twenties."

"That's my sister. Is she okay?"

With any luck the injuries would be minor.

Grant's response crushed her hopes. "No. I'm afraid she isn't. We've been searching for next of kin for most of the day. Your sister didn't carry a lot of identification on her. We found your phone number in her apartment, but there was no name."

"Never mind about that." The man's rambling was driving her crazy. She gripped her pen and tried to keep her voice level. "Please tell me what happened."

"Well…" Again he cleared his throat. "I'm sorry ma'am, but we believe your sister was caught in the path of an avalanche yesterday afternoon. At this point, we're presuming she's dead." Another pause, then he added, his voice a little rougher this time, "Both she and the man she was skiing with."

Dead. Amalie's hand went to her heart. Oh, she'd known, she'd known.

But wait one minute. "Presumed dead? Does that mean there's some chance—"

"I'm afraid not, ma'am. We haven't been able to retrieve the body, but there's no doubt Helen Fremont was skiing on that mountain when the snow released. Her backpack and personal effects have been positively identified."

"But…" Amalie remembered family vacations at Mount Tremblant, with Helena complaining about the cold, the discomfort of her downhill equipment, the long lineups to use the lifts.

"There has to be a mistake. My sister isn't the type to go skiing in dangerous mountain terrain." Still, this man had found her phone number….

Amalie dropped the pen and pressed her hand to her forehead. She was afraid she was going to burst into sobs. If only she could hold off a minute or two. While she had this man on the line, she didn't want to break down.

"Are you *sure* it was Helena on that mountain, Mr.—" she glanced at the paper "—Thorlow."

That throat-clearing business again, then he said, "Look, I realize this is a shock…"

"Yes, it is. But if you knew my sister…"

"I knew her." His voice held a quiet certainty. "I knew her, ma'am, and I can assure you there's been no mistake."

Dear God, he sounded so positive and at the same time so callous, as if he didn't *want* there to be any mistake. And the way he kept saying "ma'am" made her want to scream. *This is my sister you're talking about!*

Amalie closed her eyes, desperately seeking that old connection that would tell her Helena was alive and not buried on some distant mountain.

She felt nothing, though.

The man was right. She'd known it herself. Helena was dead.

Hearing the horrible fact was one thing. Accepting it was another. Helena dying in an avalanche was just—preposterous. This Grant Thorlow didn't seem to realize that. But this wasn't something you settled over the phone.

"I'll leave tomorrow, Mr. Thorlow." She thought of rearranging her work schedule, Davin's schooling. "Maybe Wednesday."

"You're not thinking of coming here!"

"Of course I am." God, she'd have to travel

across Ontario, through the prairies of Manitoba and Saskatchewan, then Alberta and the Rocky Mountains.

"We may not be able to recover the bodies for a while, ma'am. Conditions are—"

"You said you were calling from Rogers Pass—is there a town?"

"Golden to the east and Revelstoke to the west. Rogers Pass itself is midway between the two. There's an information center and hotel on one side of the highway and our office compound on the other. That's where I'm calling from."

"Helena's apartment—where is it?"

"Revelstoke," he said. "But—"

"I'm coming," she repeated firmly. "And I'll be bringing my nephew—"

Oh, Davin. How would he take the news? He'd never been close to Helena, of course. How could he be—they heard from her so rarely. But she *was* his mother.

"Ma'am." There was a new, hard edge to his voice. "I strongly recommend you stay home, ma'am. Roads are especially treacherous in these winter months. Besides, there's little you can do."

Amalie knew what he meant. If her sister was dead, nothing could change that. So why tackle an arduous cross-country trip?

But the alternative was staying in Toronto, never knowing exactly what had happened. She couldn't live with that. "There may not be much I can do. But I'm coming anyway."

A pause followed while he absorbed this. "Why don't you give me a call in the morning, when you've had a chance—"

"I'll call you when I get there. In about a week. And Mr. Thorlow?"

"Yeah?"

"When we meet, please don't call me ma'am. My name is Amalie."

CHAPTER TWO

"MR. THORLOW?"

Grant raised his head from his paperwork and saw the face of a dead woman. Helen Fremont.

He dropped his pen, stiffened his back and stared.

It was her—exactly. Long blond hair, even features, crystalline blue eyes. Had they made a mistake? Had she and Ramsey managed to ski out of that bowl and disappear together for over a week?

Then he saw the boy at her side. He had the same coloring as the woman, and his expression was openly curious, not particularly somber.

The nephew.

The prickles, which had danced along the skin on his face and neck, subsided. Not a ghost after all; this had to be Helen's sister.

"We were identical twins," she said. "I take it you didn't know."

Her voice was different from Helen's, not as high-pitched; or maybe it was just that she spoke slower and more quietly. One thing that was the same, however, was the slight German accent.

"No. I didn't know." But he sure as hell wished he had. He stood and offered his hand. "I'm Grant Thorlow."

"Yes." Her hand and words were cool. "I'm Amalie Fremont and this is my nephew, Davin."

He noticed the tiny emphasis she placed on her first name, and inwardly shrugged. He was aware he'd made a bad impression over the phone. But she'd been so damn unreasonable, insisting on traveling all this way, and for what?

He realized the kid was staring at him. "Hey, Davin."

"This place is totally awesome."

Amalie took a small step forward. "Davin is my sister's son."

Whoa. Helen Fremont had had a kid? He would never have guessed, had never heard anyone refer to a child.

"Officially, I'm his mother. I adopted him at birth."

Which meant Helen had deserted him at birth. Now, *that* he had no difficulty believing.

"Well, I'm sorry about your mother, Davin—and your sister." He looked back at Amalie, jolted yet again at the resemblance between the two women. And this time by the difference, as well. It was in the eyes, he decided. Helena's had been the blue of a shallow pond. Amalie's held the intensity of a deep mountain lake, glacier fed.

"We haven't heard from Helena for a while. But last I knew she was living in Seattle. I can't imagine what could have drawn her to this place."

He took the insult to his home without a blink.

"And I certainly can't picture her skiing in dangerous mountain terrain." Amalie placed her hands on his desk, her blond hair swinging forward as she leaned in toward him. "Helena was a timid person, and she was never very athletic."

Timid? Grant thought of the woman he'd seen several times in the local pub. Clearly tipsy, dressed provocatively and hanging on to the arm of first one man, then another. She'd danced with wild abandon and drawn most, if not all, eyes to the dance floor. If this Amalie wasn't so exactly like her sister, Grant might have thought they were referring to different women. He took Helen's wallet from his drawer and passed it over.

"This was your sister's."

Amalie blinked. "Where did you find it?"

"In an overnight camping hut on the Asulkan Ridge. She and Ramsey Carter skied in Saturday and spent the night there."

He swallowed, remembering the shock of finding out that it was Helen Fremont on the mountain with Ramsey, then seeing the horrible swath the avalanche had cut down the side of the mountain and knowing his friend was buried beneath it.

As if she was sharing his memories, Amalie's

face, already pale, grew whiter. She reached across the desk to open the soft, light-brown leather packet that had belonged to her sister. Inside, he knew, was only a social insurance card, a bank card and five dollars cash.

"Oh, Helena."

The whisper was laced with pain. Damn, but the woman looked ready to faint. Grant hurried around the desk to find her a chair. "Sit down. I'll get you some water."

He brought two small paper cups—one for the boy, as well. They both emptied them, while he watched, fascinated, almost freaked out by the resemblance between the two sisters.

When she was done, Amalie tossed hers in the trash. "Can you tell me what happened?"

"I can tell you what we *think* happened. We went up to investigate when Ramsey didn't return at the expected time—all overnight skiers have to register with the warden's office. Unfortunately, we weren't on the scene until about eighteen hours after the avalanche occurred."

He led her to a topographical map pinned to the wall. "Here's the Asulkan Hut, where they spent the night. Late Sunday morning we figure they traveled in this direction." He traced a path south alongside Asulkan Brook.

"They were relatively safe up on this ridge, but for some reason they approached the lip of a steep mountain bowl we call the Pterodactyl. The slope, covered in fresh-fallen snow, would've tempted an inexperienced skier.''

He crossed his arms, thinking of Ramsey, who was a doctor, not an avalanche specialist, but who'd grown up in mountain country and was definitely not inexperienced. Which meant Helen was the one who'd made the mistake, compelling Ramsey to follow after her.

''We think Helen went first,'' he said, ''triggering a hard-slab avalanche with a path length of around 1,500 meters.''

''What do you mean, hard slab?'' Davin's eyes were round.

''When the snow releases on a mountain sometimes it scatters into powder as it cascades down the slope. Other times it breaks into big chunks like the ones we saw in the debris of this avalanche. There's a lot of power behind the huge hunks of snow as they tear down those slopes. Enough power to uproot huge trees, that's for sure.''

Amalie was getting paler by the second. She reached out to her nephew, as if an arm could shelter him from the awful reality. ''But until you've found the bodies, we won't know for sure....''

The woman obviously had no idea what they were dealing with. He tried to break it to her gently. ''I've got a lot of experience with snow and mountains. Worked at Avalanche Control here at Rogers

Pass for over ten years." He leaned against the wall, folded his arms across his chest. "In my opinion, there's no doubt your sister is dead."

Along with Ramsey Carter. A good man who hadn't deserved to die.

Amalie remained skeptical. "What if someone stole Helena's wallet? Maybe she was never on that trail."

"Then why didn't she show up for work the next day?"

Amalie's gaze circled the small office. "She could have moved on."

"How would she have left? She sold her car shortly after she got here, before Christmas. We'd know if she took a bus or chartered a plane."

"Stop!"

Amalie had her hand to her forehead, and he immediately saw what an ass he was being.

"I'm sorry. I realize it can't be easy." He stared past the visitors, reminding himself it wasn't their fault Helen had been so careless, so foolish. These people were suffering, like him, like Ramsey's family.

He tried to explain. "I just don't want you to have false hopes." What they couldn't know was that he'd been through this so many times before.

"I understand." Amalie Fremont's voice sounded bleak. "But if you'd known my sister."

She'd said that to him before, during their phone

call. But he felt he *had* known her sister. At least, her type. He sat back at his desk and picked up his pen to sign the requisition forms in front of him.

Amalie returned to the chair, leaving Davin by the map. He sensed her presence as she leaned over his desk, and finally gave in and looked up. In a low voice she said, "You didn't like Helena very much, did you?"

Now, there was an understatement. He'd first met the woman shortly before Christmas, and found her flighty, brittle and insincere, qualities he detested in anyone, whether male or female.

He liked her even less now. Undoubtedly, her reckless skiing had caused that avalanche. Ramsey Carter was dead because of her.

If only she'd never passed through their quiet mountain community. Her brand of trouble belonged in the big city as far as he was concerned and he was sure plenty of others would agree with him.

As far as the twin sister went, though, he wasn't so sure. Amalie's gaze held qualities of intelligence and reserve that he'd never glimpsed in Helen. Plus there was that inexplicable buzz he'd felt from just shaking her hand. Not once had he felt that sort of attraction to Helen.

"I can't deny—"

"Is that why you won't search for her body?" Amalie pressed her finger down inches from his pen, compelling his attention. As if she didn't already have it.

"Listen, Amalie." He'd remembered not to call her ma'am, but she didn't appear too impressed.

"I *am* listening and it seems to me that if you really cared you would've done something about recovering her body days ago."

He set down his pen. "My best friend was on that mountain with your sister. If I could have done anything to save them, believe me, I would have."

"Your best friend? I'm sorry. I—I didn't realize." She closed her eyes, pressing her hands hard to her temples.

Something about the gesture got to him. He didn't like weak people and Helen had been weak. But Amalie struck him as a strong person at a vulnerable point. He wondered if she had someone to comfort her back home in Toronto. She didn't wear any rings.

Surprised by his newfound sympathy for this woman, along with his unexpected interest in her love life, Grant gave himself a mental kick in the butt. He knew where his thoughts—and his hormones—were leading him. Of all the times and of all the people... Was he trying to prove he could be as big a fool as Ramsey?

Davin came back to the desk. He'd been wandering out in the adjoining room, reading charts and examining photographs. "Wow. This place is wicked. Do you really use a howitzer to set off avalanches on purpose?''

Grant nodded. ''That's part of our program to control the snow on the mountains.''

''Awesome.''

''We have a video at the information center you ought to see if you're interested—it's called *Snow Wars*.''

Davin glanced at Amalie. ''Can we?''

She smiled indulgently. ''Of course. We'll be here long enough.''

How long? Grant wanted to ask, but figured the question would be rude. Instead, he glanced at his watch. On a normal day he'd be heading home about now. He'd have a peaceful beer by the television, then a stroll down to the local pub for a steak sandwich or maybe over to Blaine's restaurant for pizza.

''Where are you folks planning to stay?''

Amalie looked surprised by the question. ''At Helena's.''

Grant thought of the landlady he'd interviewed Monday afternoon. Heidi Eitelbach had made it clear what she'd thought of her former tenant. She wouldn't be pleased about having the sister show up on her doorstep.

''Yeah, well, your sister rented a two-bedroom apartment not far from where I live, in Revelstoke. That's a little ways farther down the highway from here. If you want to follow me in your car, I'll introduce you to the landlady. We've still got your sister's key. It was with the stuff we found at the cabin.''

He retrieved the sleeping bag and knapsack they'd brought back from the hut and tossed them to Amalie.

"Ready?" He pulled his own keys from his pocket, then shrugged into his jacket. As he led the pair through the narrow corridor, he noticed Ralph Carlson was back in his office.

"I think you should meet this guy," he told Amalie. "He works for Parks Canada and is officially in charge of any rescue mission into the backcountry."

Introductions went quickly, and Ralph reiterated Grant's own conclusion—that a recovery mission couldn't be implemented at this time.

Out in the parking lot Amalie's blue Jetta stood out in the line of four-by-four trucks. Grant was glad to see she had new-looking winter treads on her tires. Too many drivers underestimated road conditions on this stretch of the highway.

He waited as she unlocked the driver-side door. In the back seat he could see two rolled-up sleeping bags and pillows, a large cooler and stacks of books and papers.

"Is your trunk full, too?" he asked.

Amalie glanced over her shoulder to see what

he'd been looking at. It didn't take long for her to get his point. "Yes, it's full. We're planning to stay as long as it takes. I've taken a leave-of-absence from work."

"What about his schooling?" He nodded at Davin, who was just sliding into the front passenger seat.

"I'll home-school him while we're here. Thanks for your concern."

The sound of her slamming car door still rang in his ears by the time Grant reached his own truck. Obviously, he'd made a second impression even worse than the first. He supposed he hadn't come across as very sympathetic. Or very welcoming, either.

Well, that was too bad. She wasn't the only one grieving over someone. And hadn't he warned her not to come in the first place?

THE TIRES of Amalie's Jetta crunched in the snow, as she slowed and pulled over to the side of the street behind Grant Thorlow's truck. They were just two blocks from the Columbia River, on Mackenzie Avenue. The three-story apartment block was a Bavarian-styled structure of stucco and stained wood, with balconies on every unit.

A nice enough place. But Helena was a city girl. And this town—while prettier than Amalie had expected was no Toronto or Seattle.

And it was so cut off from the rest of the world. Those mountains! Amalie had never seen anything like them. She knew she ought to be impressed with their beauty, but instead she found them oppressive, frightening.

Just by Golden—the last town they'd passed before Rogers Pass—the mountains had felt like prison walls. The curves in the road had tightened, and the sheer rock face on her left had seemed close enough to touch from an open window.

The view to the right was worse—she hadn't dared look at the valley below. The short concrete guardrail had seemed to offer woefully inadequate protection against a sheer drop into nothingness.

"Is this the place?" Davin asked.

"I guess so," she said. Grant was already at the front entrance, pacing impatiently as he waited. Amalie turned to Davin. "How are you doing?"

"Sick of driving. Sick of this car." Davin got out and slammed the door behind him.

Amalie followed more slowly. Her neck and shoulders were tight from hours of concentrating on the snow-covered, winding roads, and she had a dull ache in her lower back.

Ahead, Davin ran up to Grant, his young voice raised in yet another question. Whatever he said, it made Grant laugh.

Snow had begun to fall when they were leaving the Rogers Pass compound earlier; now it covered the road with a clean white film. Amalie could see clearly the footprints of the two people who had preceded her. The smaller, even-treaded prints were from Davin's sneakers, while Grant's rugged hiking boots had left behind large, deeply grooved tracks.

She couldn't quite figure what to make of him, this Grant Thorlow. In his office, as on the phone, he'd been cool, broaching on rude. She didn't know where he got off. Did the man not have a shred of compassion in him? His stiffly offered words of sympathy about her sister's death had felt like an insult. Obviously, he wasn't happy that she'd ignored his advice and driven here, either.

It was evident that he'd disliked Helena. He'd expected to dislike her, too. The message had been plain.

Well, she'd be happy to return the favor and dislike him back.

Except... It wasn't fair that he was so ruggedly attractive. She never met men like him in the city. His features weren't anything special; he wasn't even well groomed. His hair looked as though he cut it himself, a button was missing on his faded blue shirt and his collar curled up from lack of a good ironing.

What did details like those matter, though, when a man was tall and well built, with browned, slightly ruddy skin and sharp blue-gray eyes. When Grant moved, he clearly had total command of him self, and when he spoke, his words might not be phrased tactfully, but they carried the ring of uncompromising truth.

No, in all honesty she couldn't say she disliked the man, even though he manifestly had no use for her.

"I've buzzed the landlady," Grant explained when she was almost beside him. "She should—"

He dropped the end of his sentence as a thin woman in her fifties, with sharp features and her hair up in curlers, pushed open the security door.

"Don't just stand there, Thorlow. You're letting in the cold." She stood back, surprised when not one but three of them entered the warm vestibule. Her piercing gaze skimmed right past Grant and Davin to settle on Amalie.

"Ohhh!" She sucked in a breath and stared.

One corner of Grant's mouth curled in amusement. "Identical twins." He leaned against a bank of metal mailboxes. "Heidi Eitelbach, this is Amalie Fremont. And her nephew, Davin."

Amalie stepped forward. "It's nice to meet you, Mrs. Eitelbach. My nephew and I were hoping to stay in Helena's apartment while we—while we settle my sister's affairs."

"If you're planning to settle her affairs, you can start right now." Heidi Eitelbach stamped a small slippered foot on the linoleum flooring. "Your sister was three weeks late on her rent, and if you'll be staying more than a few days, you'll have to pay for the whole next month, as well.''

Amalie hadn't counted on this. "How much?"

"Four hundred and fifty per month."

Times two. She'd have to transfer funds from her savings. Oh, Lord, what was she doing? "Fine. I'll write you a check now."

The landlady appeared surprised. "I want you to know we're real strict around here. No parties, no loud noise after ten."

"That won't be a problem."

The woman wasn't about to take her word. "Any sign of trouble and you're out. And don't think just because you have a kid—"

Was everyone in Revelstoke this callous? Amalie had to struggle to keep her tone civil. "There won't be any parties, Mrs. Eitelbach. Even if I knew anyone in this town—which I don't—my sister has just died. I'm hardly about to start celebrating."

Grant intervened quickly. "Amalie has a key, Heidi. I'll take her and the boy up, then come back with your check."

"Don't let her sweet-talk you out of it." Heidi pointed a finger at Grant's chest. Right about the spot where that button was missing.

"I won't." Grant opened the door to the stairwell. "Up one floor."

Amalie followed Davin, with Grant behind them both. The landlady had been downright rude, and not a word of condolence about her sister's death. Obviously, she shared at least some of Grant's antipathy toward Helena.

A sudden urge to cry was almost overwhelming. Amalie faltered and grabbed at the railing.

"You okay?" Right away Grant was beside her, and she wondered how he could be concerned about her tripping on the stairs, when he didn't seem to care a whit about her sister's death.

He put a hand under her elbow as she regained her balance. Lord, he was big. His presence loomed like the mountains. Solid. Unyielding.

And very masculine.

"I'm fine." She picked up her pace, despite the pounding of her heart, which had accelerated rather than abated during her brief pause.

At the top landing, Grant gave directions again. "First door on the right."

Davin rushed in as soon as Amalie twisted the key. She let him go ahead, while she hesitated on the threshold with Grant.

"This is just a hunch, but I'm guessing Mrs. Eitelbach didn't care much for my sister, either."

Grant leaned against the wall on the opposite side of the hall. His posture was relaxed, but Amalie felt that he was watching her keenly.

"She's a sharp old bird," he said, "but she didn't mean any harm. She had a lot to put up with."

Amalie pulled her checkbook out of her purse, then searched for her ballpoint pen. "I suppose you mean from Helena?"

His gaze unwavering, he didn't say a word.

Quickly, Amalie wrote out the check for nine hundred dollars, unable to stop her hand from shaking as she added her signature. It was so much money. Her parents would really think she was crazy if they knew.

When she was done, she contemplated her companion. The hall light overhead cast long shadows across the lower portion of his face. She noticed a mark now, under his bottom lip, where he might have cut himself shaving that morning.

"Just what is it you have against my sister? What did she ever do to you?"

Grant stepped away from the wall. "It's not so much what she did to me as what she did to my friend."

"Oh?"

"The man she was skiing with?"

She tried to remember. "Ramsey—"

"Ramsey Carter." The name came out short, clipped with anger. "My best friend. My *married* best friend."

Amalie stared at him. "You can't mean—"

"Your sister was having an affair with a married man. Now he's dead, and his widow will have to raise their two children on her own."

Grant took her check, holding it between his thumb and forefinger gingerly, as if it were something he'd rather not touch.

"That's *one* of the things I have against your sister."

CHAPTER THREE

HELENA'S APARTMENT WAS A SHOCK. Amalie stood with her back to the closed door—Grant Thorlow's final words still echoing in her ears—and surveyed the scene.

"Kind of weird, isn't it?" Davin said. He'd turned on the television and was manually searching the channels. "I mean, there's nothing here. Not even a lamp."

It was true; the only illumination came from a bare bulb in the center of the ceiling. An old sofa—the kind you might see discarded at the side of a curb—was against the long wall of the living room. Opposite was a small TV, sitting directly on the stained, tan carpet.

"I guess Helena didn't have much money." Or maybe she hadn't planned on staying very long.

Amalie set down her purse, then followed the short hallway to the right. Here was the bathroom and two bedrooms. The first was empty; the second was obviously Helena's. On the floor was an old mattress, the bedding scattered and wrinkled.

An old oak dresser stood in the corner, next to

the open doors of a closet. Eager to find something, anything, that would connect this place with the fastidious sister she remembered, Amalie opened the drawers of the bureau, but here, too, all was a jumble.

Automatically, she started sorting and folding, only pausing when the lush wool of one sweater had her peeking at the label. Cashmere, sure enough, from a designer Amalie had seen advertised in fashion magazines.

Intrigued, Amalie checked over the rest of the clothing. Interspersed with regular, department store items, the kind she normally bought for herself, she found a couple more treasures—a beautiful hand-knit sweater, some silk lingerie.

In the closet, the same dichotomy was evident. Mixed in with a beautiful Anne Klein suit and butter-soft leather pants were no-brand jeans and cotton T-shirts.

Probably the less-expensive items had been purchased here in Revelstoke, but it was the high-end clothing that most puzzled Amalie. Presumably, money had once not been a problem for her sister— an hypothesis borne out by the contents of the carved wooden box that sat on top of the bureau. Once opened, it released a delicate scent of sandalwood and light chimes played ''My Favorite Things,'' from *The Sound of Music*.

Amalie smiled, remembering the first time she'd

watched the musical with her sister, on an outing to the theater with some friends. Their mother had been livid when she found out. Strictly speaking, dancing was forbidden by their church, and the sight of her daughters whirling and singing around the living room had prompted her to ground them for an extended period.

Their parents' religious doctrines had been such a confining presence in their lives. Amalie knew that Helena in particular had resented it. She herself, however, still found them a comfort, although in her heart she took significantly more moderate views from those of her parents and their minister.

Inside the carved box were little velvet bags. Amalie selected one and pulled the silk cord gently. Out tumbled a gold ring with a sapphire as big as her thumbnail. Gasping, Amalie put it back in the bag, then checked another.

This time she found a short gold chain strung with diamonds. Where had Helena found the money for this jewelry? Or had they been gifts...?

Amalie shut the lid on the ornate box and was about to turn away, when she noticed a small indentation next to a carved rose at the bottom of the case. She picked the box up and worked the nail of her index finger into the hollow. A small drawer sprang out from the bottom. Inside was a pouch of dried grass and several sheets of thin white paper

Amalie didn't have to smell the one rolled cigarette to know what she'd found.

She pulled the drawer out from the case and carried it to the bathroom. One flush, and the marijuana was gone. The papers she threw in the trash.

Amalie returned to the bedroom, pushed the drawer back into the box, then shoved the whole thing underneath a pile of Helena's lingerie.

As far as she knew, Helena had never used drugs when she'd lived on her own in Toronto. And certainly not when she was still at home with their parents. Alcohol and tobacco had been major taboos. Drugs were unthinkable.

So when had Helena changed, and why hadn't Amalie sensed the changes from the occasional letters and phone calls that had tenuously linked them over the years?

Amalie closed the bedroom door behind her and went to check on Davin, who remained transfixed in front of the television.

"Are you hungry?" she asked.

"Yeah." He nodded, his eyes not leaving the screen.

An open doorway to the left gave access to a small galley kitchen. She was relieved to see the counters and stovetop were clean. Beside the fridge, though, stacks of empty beer and wine bottles brought back Mrs. Eitelbach's admonishment: "No parties. No loud music."

After toeing a case of Kootenay Mountain Ale out of the way first, Amalie opened the fridge, then checked the cupboards. Not much to choose from, except boxes of macaroni and cheese.

Amalie smiled. She'd forgotten how Helena had loved these. Just like Davin.

She pulled out a package, then put water on to boil. There was milk in the fridge, but it had gone bad. She would have to mix the dried cheese sauce with water and a little margarine. First thing tomorrow she'd go shopping.

Amalie set the table, picturing yet more dollars flying out from her savings account. This trip was going to cost her much more than she'd expected, putting her goal of owning a house even further into the future.

And yet she couldn't regret having come. Despite all the disturbing reports she was getting about her sister. Or maybe *because* of them.

THE NEXT DAY Amalie cleaned the apartment and stocked the cupboards and refrigerator with enough food to last a couple of weeks. She stopped at the local hardware store to pick up a few items, including a foam mattress for Davin's sleeping bag.

A phone call to her parents, after dinner, confirmed their opinion about this trip.

"You're wasting your time and money," her father said, on the upstairs extension.

"And what about your job and Davin's education?" her mother asked.

"I've taken a leave of absence from the hospital and I talked with Davin's teacher before we left. I'm going to make sure he keeps up with the curriculum." The sound of shattering glass had her twisting toward the kitchen counter. Davin had been drying the dishes and a bowl had slipped from his fingers to the floor.

She covered the mouthpiece. "That's okay, hon. I'll clean it up later. Why don't you go in the living room. It's almost time for your program."

Back on the phone, her parents were wondering how long they'd hold her job at the hospital with the way she was behaving.

"Frankly, I don't even care right now. You have no idea how Helena was living here, Mom. She had barely anything in her apartment." Except drugs and beer.

It still didn't make sense to Amalie. At twenty-nine, she'd assumed her sister had been making something of her life. Although she'd never given specifics, Helena's letters had hinted at jobs, friends, a normal existence.

"Look, Mom, Dad, I've got to go. Davin needs my help. I'll call back in a few days and tell you what's happening."

She hung up from the duty call with relief, then went to the cupboard for the broom and dustpan.

Just as she was dumping the smashed glass into the garbage, the phone rang.

No doubt her parents. What had they forgotten to warn her about?

But it was Grant Thorlow on the line. Immediately, she was on her guard. The man's brusque manner had definitely wounded yesterday. And yet, she couldn't say she was sorry to hear his voice again.

"I was wondering if Davin would like a tour of the Avalanche Control Center tomorrow. He seemed pretty interested in our program the other day. Plus there's that video I was telling you about..."

Snow Wars, she remembered, impressed by the offer but slightly suspicious, as well. Why was he suddenly being so nice? "That's very kind of you."

"Yeah, well..." He cleared his throat. "I didn't mean to be rude yesterday. Especially in front of the kid."

Amalie's opinion of the man went up a notch at his apology. She liked people who had soft spots for children. "I guess you *were* pretty plainspoken, but I came here wanting the truth about Helena."

There was a pause on the other end of the line. Then his voice, a little more tentative this time. "Are you sure about that? Maybe you and the boy are better off not knowing...."

Amalie felt a buzz of anxiety. "Not knowing what?"

"Nothing. It's just that you two seem like nice people."

"And so was Helena." Amalie turned to face the wall, lowering her voice so Davin couldn't hear her above the sound of the television in the next room.

"She may have made some bad choices in her life, but basically Helena was a good person."

"A good person?" Grant's incredulity was clear, even over the phone. "Look, she was your sister, and you can believe what you want. But if it wasn't for her, Ramsey Carter would still be alive today. Denise Carter would still have a husband. Her kids would have a father."

There was something so inherently unfair about Grant's judgment. Amalie twisted the telephone cord and fought for self-control. "It works both ways. Nobody *forced* Ramsey Carter to go up that mountain with Helena. Did it ever occur to you that the ski trip could have been Ramsey's idea? That it might be *his* fault that Helena died?"

"THERE ARE OVER 130 avalanche slidepaths that intersect with the Trans-Canada Highway along the Rogers Pass route through the Selkirk Mountains," Grant told Davin later the next day, after Amalie and Davin had sat through the *Snow Wars* video in the information center theater.

He was still a little angry with himself. Even though he'd claimed to have arranged this outing for Davin's sake—he knew the truth. He'd wanted to see Amalie again.

"Maybe some parts of the world aren't meant to be lived in," she said now, studying a picture of the 105 mm howitzer used to trigger avalanches in designated situations.

"The trains need to travel through the mountains somehow," Grant said quietly. "So do motorists. This corridor was the best available."

"But it's so *dangerous*." Despite her thick wool sweater, Amalie looked chilled. She hugged her arms around her body, her gaze caught by the view from the glass entranceway. She didn't seem to appreciate the scenery.

"Yes, it's dangerous," Grant agreed. "In an average year we have about 1,500 slides along this highway. Can you imagine how many are happening out in the wilderness?"

Davin whistled. "But you control the avalanches, don't you, Mr. Thorlow? With the howitzer."

"That's my job, but avalanche control is hardly an exact science." Grant shoved his hands into his dark-blue nylon pants. Amalie had moved on to another exhibit.

Don't stare, man! This is one woman who's definitely off-limits.

"We monitor air temperature, wind speed and

direction, precipitation and relative humidity," he continued. "Then we perform field tests to check the layers in the snowpack. But people who think they can predict the timing and size of an avalanche with certainty are just kidding themselves. Even the avalanches we trigger intentionally sometimes surprise the heck out of us."

"Why are there so many avalanches on this part of the highway?" Davin asked, his attention on a large model of the mountain pass that dominated the main room of the information center.

"Steep slopes, lots of snow." Grant shrugged. "Those are the basic ingredients."

Amalie was now walking around the three-dimensional replica of the mountain pass. She was about to ask him a question, when he noticed someone at the main doors.

Denise Carter stood there, her brown hair tied back in a ponytail and cheeks pink from the cold. She spotted him right away and he stepped forward to engulf her in a hug.

"Denise. How are you? How are the kids?"

She shook her head at the first question, only answering the second. "The kids are coping... Mom and Dad are with them." She leaned into his chest, crumbling like powered snow in a harmless sluff.

And then she noticed Amalie.

"Helen?" First shock, then hatred transformed her features and stiffened her body.

"No. I'm her twin sister. Amalie Fremont."

"You didn't tell me Helen had a sister. That she would be coming... That she looked so much like..." Denise glared at Grant as if he'd betrayed her in some way.

"Amalie lives in Toronto. I didn't expect her to travel all this way." Grant began explanations, then halted. "I'm sorry, Denise. I should have prepared you. I was shocked, too, the first time I saw her."

Amalie had her hands to her face, as if trying to conceal the features that reminded them all of a different woman.

"You shouldn't have come here." Denise made a move toward Amalie, whipping off her mitten to point her finger.

"Denise." Grant took hold of her arm. "There's someone else you should know about. A child. His name is Davin."

At the sound of his name, Davin glanced up from the model. "Hi there," he said uncertainly, eyeing the peculiar expression on this new stranger's face.

Denise looked back at Amalie. "Your son?"

"I adopted him and raised him from birth," she answered. "But he's really...he's really Helena's child."

"Helen had a child?" She whipped around to Grant. "Did you know this?"

He shook his head. "It doesn't matter, Denise. Come on, let me take you home. Or maybe you'd like to go have a cup of coffee. We can—"

Denise shook off his hand. Spinning back to Amalie, she pointed her finger once again.

"Ramsey was a good husband until he met your sister!"

In a flash, anger became despair. Denise began to sob. Grant pulled her against his body, but his gaze stayed on Amalie.

YOU SHOULDN'T HAVE COME. Amalie read the message in Grant's face as clearly as if he'd spoken the words.

Helena was a person, too! she wanted to cry back at both him and Denise. Her sister deserved to be mourned, deserved to be missed, deserved to be cared about.

Remembering Davin, Amalie reached for the boy and wrapped her arm around his shoulder. He was staring at the crying woman, watching as Grant urged her out the door and into his truck.

"Why does everyone hate Helena so much?" he asked finally. "Was she a bad person?"

Resentment tightened Amalie's chest as she turned her back to the door, to the people who had just left. True, Denise was in pain, but she was a mother, too. How could she have said such things in front of Davin?

"They just didn't know her, Davin. That's all."
She gave him a hug and made a second, silent deduction.

And neither did I.

CHAPTER FOUR

"YOU KNOW RAMSEY was in the middle of reno-
vating our basement, don't you?" Denise asked.

She'd stopped crying at last. Now she was sitting
in Grant's living room, holding the cup of tea he'd
made her out of desperation. He hadn't known
where else to take her. She hadn't wanted to go
home, couldn't face a restaurant. So he'd brought
her here.

Grant was prepared for a lot of emergencies.
He'd led many a search-and-rescue operation, could
provide basic first aid better than many doctors and
had even survived a couple of unexpected encoun-
ters with grizzly bears.

But what to do with a crying woman? That
wasn't one of his fortes.

Now he sat on the very edge of his reclining
chair and thought about the question Denise asked.
Of course he'd known Ramsey was finishing the
basement of the house he shared with Denise and
their two children, Colin and Chrissy. He'd helped
Ramsey haul in a load of drywall two weekends
ago.

"What am I going to do, Grant? I've got a half-finished basement I can't afford to hire someone to complete, mortgage payments due every month and two children who adored their father and can't understand why he was out skiing with a woman when he told us he was going to be working on a special assignment."

The pain in Denise's eyes was too naked to look at. Grant cleared his throat and glanced instead at the cup in his hand. He thought about the issues she'd raised, and picked the easiest to deal with.

"Don't worry about money. There'll be insurance." Ramsey was the type to have arranged provisions for his family. Which only made his death that much more of a puzzle. What *was* he doing out on that mountain with Helen Fremont? Had the man totally lost his mind?

To Grant, it was incomprehensible. Especially considering the flak Ramsey had always given him about getting a wife, having some kids. Apparently, family life wasn't as idyllic as Ramsey had made it out to be.

"I can't believe he took her there, to the Asulkan Hut." Denise's mouth twisted bitterly. "That's where we went the day he asked me to marry him. It was his special place, *our* special place. Whenever he had an important decision..."

She choked back a sob, took a stabilizing breath.

"Did you know, Grant? That he was seeing that woman?"

He was relieved that he could honestly shake his head no. "I didn't have a clue."

No one had been more surprised than him to find out Helen Fremont had accompanied Ramsey to that mountain retreat. The two of them had obviously spent Saturday night together. And the ramifications were now tearing Denise apart.

Grant, too, felt betrayed. Ramsay had lied to him, as well as to Denise, concealing a relationship that went against every principle the young doctor had presumably believed in.

"Who's going to take Colin to his hockey games now?" Denise asked, more tears pooling in her eyes. "My car needs an oil change—Ramsey was supposed to do that last weekend...."

Grant's impulse was to tell her he would do all these chores. He'd finish the basement; he'd drive Colin to his games; he'd service the cars and do whatever else had to be done. After all, he'd been Ramsey's closest friend. Ramsey would expect him to help his family. And Grant would be happy to do so.

But something told him Denise was looking for more than a handyman to help pick up the pieces. She needed emotional support, a confidant. He wasn't so sure he could fit that role. Watching her cry now was so hard. He just didn't know what to *say*.

"Is your tea sweet enough? Can I get you anything to eat?" In the freezer he had some miniature pizzas he could heat in the microwave.

"The tea is fine. I'm not hungry." Denise leaned closer toward him, setting her cup down on the plank table between them.

"You've been such a good friend, Grant. I really appreciate having your shoulder to cry on. I can't talk to the kids, obviously, and my parents are too old for me to burden with my heartache. I told them Ramsey was skiing with someone from work. Fortunately, they haven't heard any of the gossip that must be circulating around town."

While Grant had cautioned the initial rescue party to keep details of the situation private, he had to agree that there would be talk anyway. It was unavoidable in a town the size of Revelstoke.

"Seeing her sister this afternoon at the center— for a moment I thought it was Helen. That she'd somehow survived."

"I know. I had the same reaction when she came into the office yesterday." The resemblance was uncanny. And yet, already he'd stopped seeing Helen when he looked at Amalie. There *was* a difference, in the way she carried herself, the way she spoke....

Much as he'd been predisposed to dislike the

woman, it was impossible. She had a certain dignity that made him feel guilty whenever he said something particularly harsh about her sister. Still, she claimed she wanted the truth about Helen, so he wasn't about to sugarcoat the facts.

"You've told her it's too dangerous to recover the b-bodies?"

"I have."

"Then she'll be leaving soon?"

The look in Denise's eyes was almost pleading. Grant wished he could reassure her. "I can't say. My impression is she plans to stay until we can go in there."

"But that could be weeks, even months!"

Grant shrugged. He realized that. But what could he do?

Denise's gaze slid off to the side, her mouth set in a bitter line.

"I'm sorry for all you're going through, Denise. You and the kids meant the world to Ramsey. I know you did. Helen…" Grant cast his eyes about the room, searching for words that never came easily in the best of circumstances.

"She was nothing, compared with you and the kids," he said finally. "Ramsey would have straightened out. I'm sure he would've."

"For me right now, that's the hardest part. Not knowing if Ramsey really did love me. How am I supposed to mourn a man who was cheating on me, Grant? Can you tell me that?''

He shook his head. No, he couldn't tell her that.

Denise was crying again, behind cover of her hands. Feeling awkward, Grant moved closer and stroked her shoulder. Before he knew it, her face was tucked against his chest, her arms were clutching him desperately. The sobs came out so harshly now he was afraid she might get sick.

''Shh, shh...'' God, he felt so helpless.

''You would never do something like that to a woman, would you, Grant?''

Denise's breath was hot and moist against his ear, and Grant felt a sweat of his own break out on his brow.

''I could change your oil for you, Denise. I have time right now, if you like.''

She stilled in his arms. After about a minute, she lifted her head and examined his face.

He felt too embarrassed to meet her eyes. ''And why don't I come round and case out your basement. There's probably not as much work left as you think.''

Denise brushed the hair at the side of his head with her hand. ''You're a very good-looking man, Grant. I've always thought that about you.''

''Thanks. So are you. A beautiful woman, I mean.'' It seemed like the right thing to say, although Grant had never viewed Denise in that way and really had no opinion on the matter. She was the wife of a good friend. That had been enough.

"Why don't I get you home now, before your parents start to worry." Then he remembered her vehicle was still at the information center. "I'll get one of the guys to help me bring your Jeep back after I change the oil."

Somehow, he'd eased them both into a standing position. Now he bent to retrieve the cups from the table and carried them to the dishwasher. When he came back, she had her coat on and was picking up her purse.

That was good. He started to whistle, then stopped when his lips were too stiff to cooperate. Swallowing quickly, he pulled his truck keys out of his coat pocket and then opened the door for her. On the way out, she managed a weak smile.

He felt an instant tug of sympathy. For all she had lost, for all she had left to face. And his anger toward Helen Fremont flared higher. They would have all been so much better off if she'd never moved to town.

And he'd never met her sister, Amalie.

From the moment he'd found out she intended to come to Rogers Pass, Grant had expected Amalie to be a thorn in his side. Pressuring him to mount a recovery mission before the mountain had stabilized; reminding him, by her very presence, of the woman who'd caused all this trouble in the first place.

Instead, he found himself sympathizing for her position. And undeniably attracted. Reactions he couldn't justify to himself, let alone Denise. He knew his loyalties had to lie with the people of this town. Yet he also knew that before too long, he would find another excuse to see her again.

"I DO FEEL BAD for Denise," Amalie said. She dropped her spoon in the mug of hot chocolate and looked cautiously at Grant, who was sitting in the opposite kitchen chair.

He'd dropped in late, after Davin was already in bed. Ostensibly here to apologize for Denise Carter's behavior at the information center yesterday, he'd done nothing but justify it.

"I know you don't agree," Amalie continued, "but it isn't fair for everyone to place all the blame on Helena. After all—" she lifted her spoon to emphasize the point "—he *was* the married one."

Grant didn't appear convinced. "He was such a steady guy. A real family man. He wouldn't have strayed unless he was sorely tempted."

"Davin was devastated. Denise said some pretty ugly things." That was the part she just couldn't forgive. She understood the other woman's anger. But in front of a child...

"There may be other ugly scenes to come. You

know, you could always leave and he wouldn't have to face them.''

Amalie was reminded of what Grant had said to her the other night in the hallway. How Helena's affair with Ramsey had been *one* of the reasons he hadn't liked her.

''Are you warning me off?''

''Not exactly,'' he said. Then changed his mind. ''Hell, yes. I'm warning you off. As I tried to explain on the phone, there's nothing you can do here. Your sister's dead and that's not going to change... whether we pull out the bodies tomorrow, next week or after spring thaw!''

''Spring thaw?'' Amalie thought of her financial situation and shuddered. ''Could it really take that long?''

''It might.'' He slanted her an appraising look. ''Are you prepared to wait it out? And what about Davin? Besides missing school, he's going to have to face what the townspeople will say about your sister. And I'm warning you, a lot of it won't be pretty.''

Amalie refused to listen. Grant was biased against Helena. Absentmindedly, she stirred the cocoa again, melancholy slowing her motions. She and her sister hadn't been close in years, but it was so hard to think that she was gone now. Forever.

''Well, I can see I won't change your mind.'' Grant sounded disappointed.

"That's what you really came here for, isn't it?" Not to apologize but to ask her to leave. And she'd thought he'd been worried about her and Davin. Which had been foolish of her. His allegiance would remain with the people from this town. People like Denise Carter.

"Your leaving would help smooth things over."

For Denise, it would. And maybe, in the short term, for her and Davin, too. But in the long run, the questions would surely drive them crazy. They'd never know how Helena had ended up in Rogers Pass, why she appeared to have been hooked on drugs and alcohol, how she'd come to the point where she'd been having an affair with a married man. There had to be explanations for these things; people didn't just change for no reason.

"I owe it to Davin to find out the truth about his mother. About her life, as well as her death."

"Why? He seems more interested in my work than in what happened to Helen. He didn't even know her, right?"

Amalie bristled under the implied criticism. "They corresponded. Occasionally," she had to confess.

"Corresponded?" Grant's eyebrows rose in dark, arched lines. "Did she ever visit him?"

No, she never had. Not once in eleven years. It wasn't something Amalie herself understood, but then, they'd never gone searching for Helena, either.

"Grant, she was his mother and my sister. We can't just shrug and return to Toronto as if she never mattered."

He understood. She saw the flash of sympathy in his eyes in the second before he turned away from her. In that instant she realized he wasn't cold and unfeeling but a man torn by conflicting loyalties. Which made it easier for her to disregard his next statement.

"It isn't going to be pleasant for you. You're not going to like some of the things you find out."

Amalie didn't see how the situation could get much worse. "We'll deal with that if it happens."

Grant's gaze was suddenly personal. "You're very determined. Stubborn."

There was grudging respect behind his assessment. And even a gleam of admiration in his eyes. She was unexpectedly driven to explain herself.

"I feel that I owe Helena. I've always had it easy. She's the one who was dealt all the tough breaks."

"What do you mean?"

"Growing up with my parents...they're good people, but they were rigid in their expectations." Partly due to their religion and partly because they'd never lost the fear that this new, free country might somehow corrupt their daughters.

"Oh?"

"Nothing Helena ever did could please my mother. While I—" she shrugged disparagingly "—I could seem to do no wrong. It wasn't fair and it only got worse when Helena announced she was pregnant."

"With Davin?"

She nodded. "My parents were furious. To them, pregnancy outside of marriage was a woman's ultimate disgrace. Unforgivable. Besides being ostracized, Helena also had to cope with severe medical problems. Believe me, she suffered terribly."

"She deserted her son once he was born."

His stark judgment proved he didn't understand. Amalie wasn't surprised. He couldn't realize that when their mother had told Helena she wasn't capable of raising a child on her own, Helena had *believed* her.

Grant rubbed his face. He looked beat. Amalie remembered him telling Davin his day started at 4:30 in the morning. It was close to ten at night now. "It's late. You must be exhausted."

"No, I'm fine," he said, but the physical evidence was to the contrary. As he fought back another yawn, she took their empty mugs to the sink.

He watched for a moment, then eventually he rose, too, looming large in Helena's tiny kitchen. She dropped the dishrag, aware of his broad shoulders, barrel chest and powerful arms. Solid muscle, all of him. No wonder Denise had fallen against him for support. He was definitely up for it.

"You're right. I'd better go." His voice rasped in the quiet of the apartment.

Amalie turned, caught his gaze, and was surprised at what she saw in his eyes. Something tender she hadn't noticed before. And intense. Almost as if...

But no, he *couldn't* be attracted to her. True, they'd exchanged a few unsettling looks this evening. But they hadn't meant anything....

"Amalie?" He took a step forward, not breaking eye contact.

She had to fight not to hold out her hands to him. When his gaze dropped to her mouth, she guessed he was wondering what it would be like to kiss her.

She turned away, knowing she was being foolish, that she *had* to be imagining his interest in her. He didn't even like her—well, maybe he'd softened a little since their first meeting, but that hardly constituted—

"Are you serious about delving into your sister's life?"

The question startled her, but her answer came quickly. "Yes, I am."

"Tomorrow's Friday. I could take you to the bar where she used to work. You could talk to some of the people there."

"Helena worked in a bar?"

"Yeah. The Rock Slide Saloon."

The name made her smile. "Yes, I'd like to go check it out."

He moved a few inches closer. Maybe she hadn't imagined that spark between them. For a moment it seemed he truly would kiss her. This time she resolved she wasn't going to back away at the last minute.

But he surprised her by speaking, instead.

"I still think you should return to Toronto."

The warning was mitigated by a new warmth in his smile.

"And I say I'm staying."

"Then it's a date? Tomorrow at the Rock Slide Saloon?"

"Yes." A date with Grant Thorlow. She never would've guessed the evening would end like this.

DAVIN LISTENED TO THE SOUND of the door closing, then the scrape of metal as his aunt turned the dead bolt.

He rolled over in his sleeping bag, careful to stay on the foam pad underneath him.

So Grant was gone. Too bad he'd come so late. Davin had gotten up once for a drink of water, hoping his aunt would invite him to stay and visit, but they'd both been quiet until he went back to his room.

What had they talked about? He hadn't heard their words, only the murmur of their voices.

But it was probably Helena. Everyone seemed to want to talk about her around here. And no one had much good to say.

Aunt Amalie kept telling him it was because folks didn't know her. But Davin was beginning to think maybe everyone here *did* know Helena. It was his aunt who was wrong.

Helena had been a bad person. That's what Grant thought. And so did the woman who'd been crying at the information center yesterday.

Davin agreed. Leaving your kid to be raised by your sister wasn't normal. He'd figured that much out in kindergarten.

Sometimes he wished Aunt Amalie had never told him about Helena. He wished she'd just pretended he was hers, and they could be like a regular family and he could call her Mom, which was what she was, after all.

More than Helena, that was for sure. A mother wasn't someone who wrote a letter or sent a present sometimes, only when she felt like it. And always something the wrong size or a toy he wasn't interested in.

Some nights he made up stories to get himself to sleep. He imagined his aunt coming into his room and explaining that it was all a mistake. She really was his mother, and that woman who wrote the letters and stuff was his aunt.

Only it wasn't that way.

Helena was his mother and now she was dead, and he didn't even care.

Davin stared up at the ceiling, remembering his aunt calling him to their kitchen in Toronto to tell him about the avalanche, to explain that they had to drive to Rogers Pass.

At first he'd been excited. They were going on a trip, and he was going to miss school. It had seemed like an adventure, setting out to find where his mother had lived and what she'd been like.

And it had been exciting to meet Grant and to learn about the awesome stuff they did to control the avalanches around here.

But this apartment—it was so weird it was spooky, the way Helena didn't seem to have owned anything. He and Aunt Amalie didn't have much money, either, but their house was warm and cozy, with all the regular stuff most other people had, like cushions and chairs, lamps and pictures.

That was another thing. There were no photographs in this place. A few times they'd had a box number to write to, and his aunt had included several photographs with his thank-you letters for her presents. He'd always imagined Helena would have his picture stuck to her fridge, or maybe in a frame by her bed. Now he knew Helena had probably chucked them out as soon as she got them.

CHAPTER FIVE

"Aw, AUNTY, this China stuff sucks!" Davin tossed down his pencil and crossed his arms. "I don't want to study about some country on the other side of the world."

Amalie felt a tug of sympathy. "But Davin, it's part of the curriculum."

"I don't care. Why can't I research something interesting?"

"Such as?" Amalie bent to pick up the pencil that had rolled onto the floor.

"Avalanches!" Davin twisted his head so he could see out the window, where a thick coating of snow covered every object in sight.

Living in Toronto, they were used to snow, but not in these quantities. Yesterday Grant had told them that Glacier National Park had received the greatest recorded average yearly snowfall in Canada, and she believed it.

At least the temperatures weren't as cold as on the prairies, but even this was a mixed blessing. It was the westerly flow of mild, humid air that created the unstable snow layers that eventually caused avalanches.

"You want to study avalanches instead of China?" Strange how a subject that frightened her so was fascinating to Davin.

Of course, he hadn't experienced what she had the day of Jeremy's party. The memory of Helena's suffering was a constant companion. That feeling of suffocation, the terror of not being able to suck in a breath of air... Getting caught in an avalanche was a horrific way to die.

"What do you have in mind?" she asked.

"I want to do a report on what causes them and how dangerous they are, and on Grant's job of trying to manage them. I could take pictures and do research at the information center. And I bet Grant would answer all my questions if he knew it was for a school project."

Amalie was amused at Davin's earnestness. Grant would answer his questions under any circumstances, she was sure. He'd already demonstrated such patience with the young boy.

"I promised your teacher we'd follow the curriculum."

Davin's excited grin faded, and his gaze settled on the table surface. "But I don't care about this stuff," he reiterated, pushing aside the book from the local library.

Amalie reconsidered. Enthusiasm ought to count

for something. And the project would teach him important research skills. "Well, maybe we could make an exception in this one subject area. If you promise to keep up with all the others."

"Oh, yeah!" Davin jumped up from his chair, giving her a high-five.

"Especially literature," she stressed. "One book report every week."

Davin rolled his eyes, but even that piece of news couldn't wipe the smile from his face. "This will be so sweet. The kids at school are going to be so impressed."

"We can start on your research tomorrow. I thought we'd take a break from studying now and have lunch. Is there anything you'd like to do this afternoon?"

"Could we try cross-country skiing in the mountains?"

Davin's answer dismayed her.

"Are you sure you wouldn't rather check out the town? Maybe we could catch an afternoon matinee, if there are any good movies playing."

"We can watch a movie anytime. I want to go exploring." Davin pushed back from the table. "We can rent the equipment, Aunty. We wouldn't have to buy anything."

His automatic concern for her finances gave her a pang. "Well, there are probably some safe, groomed trails we could try."

"Let's go to the information center and ask," he suggested.

The information center. Perhaps Grant Thorlow would be there. Suddenly, Davin's idea for an outing was a little more appealing.

ON THEIR WAY OUT to the car, Amalie and Davin ran into Heidi Eitelbach. Their landlady was carrying a stack of newspapers, and Davin stepped forward to help without being asked. Amalie followed them to the basement, where Heidi had the recycling containers arranged in a neat row.

Today their landlady was dressed in long pants and a top that looked like pajamas. They were purple and fuzzy, and she had her hair in curlers and her feet in suede slippers.

She stood with her hands on her hips once the papers were properly sorted and regarded the two of them.

"Well. Where are you off to today?" she asked, eyeing Amalie's wool-lined, brown suede coat.

The coat had been a splurge, purchased at fifty percent off last spring. Amalie was wearing it with a matching pair of brown cords and a cream-colored turtleneck.

"We thought we'd check into cross-country skiing. I was hoping to rent some equipment today, then go out tomorrow. Could you recommend a shop?"

Heidi's pale eyes sparked. "After what happened to your sister, I would have thought you'd steer clear of our mountains."

Amalie's own reservations skyrocketed, but she fought to remain logical. "We're certainly not going into the backcountry. We just thought we'd try a safe little trail and get some exercise."

Heidi nodded, although her eyes gleamed with mischief. She gave Amalie the name of a store that would rent them equipment, then touched her arm as they prepared to leave.

"There was a terrible accident back in '93 on the Bruins Pass. I'd stay clear of it, if I were you."

Amalie nodded and turned for the door, but Davin had stopped in his tracks.

"What happened?" His blue eyes were wide with fascination.

"Well..." Heidi leaned against the concrete wall, making herself comfortable. Amalie prepared herself for a bit of a wait.

"It was two men out skiing together that time. March 17 it happened, but believe me there was no sign of green on the mountains that day. Avalanche danger was high and just two days previous we'd had about twenty-five centimeters of fresh snow."

"Is that bad?" Davin asked, his eyes riveted on the older lady.

"Oh sure. Sometimes a heavy snowfall itself can trigger an avalanche," Heidi replied. "Anyway, one of the lads wanted to call it a day, but the other one wouldn't let him. So they kept climbing until they reached about twenty-five hundred meters.''

"Wow!"

"They were at opposite ends of a horizontal path across the mountain, when the lead skier—this was the guy who'd refused to quit—hit a weak pillow of snow. His weight triggered the avalanche, but both men were caught up in it.''

"Then what happened?'' Davin and Amalie asked simultaneously.

"Well, the second guy, the fellow who'd wanted to quit—he was smart. He released his bindings, threw off his pack and poles and swam through the snow. When it was over, he'd traveled about three hundred meters and was still on the surface.''

"And the other guy?'' Davin asked, breathlessly.

"Not so lucky.'' Heidi buffed the newspapers' black ink from her hands onto the legs of her pajamas. "He was able to throw off his poles, but he had the safety straps on his skis and the bindings wouldn't release.''

"Oh, my Lord.'' Amalie thought of Helena and felt behind herself for something stable to lean against. She found the security of a wall and continued to listen as Heidi carried on with her tale.

"The one thing they'd done right was to wear transceivers. The surviving guy started searching right away, and finally located a signal about eight hundred meters down the hill. By the time he dug the fellow out, about fifteen minutes had passed.''

''And?''

''It was too late. He signaled for help, then tried to resuscitate his partner for over half an hour, but it did no good.''

Davin gulped. ''He died?''

''He died,'' Heidi confirmed. ''Now, you two be real careful out there. Stick to the trail, you hear? And remember to wear transceivers.''

HEIDI'S STORY WAS an unneeded warning for Amalie, who was already terrified about tackling the snow on these mountains. But hearing about the skiing tragedy was good for Davin, reminding him that he wasn't as invincible as he thought.

''Why do you suppose those guys went out on the mountain when they knew it was dangerous?'' he asked Amalie.

She had no answer. But she did find it odd that in some respects his reaction to the story Heidi had told them had been more emotional than his response to the news about his mother.

Maybe because his mother had been such a distant figure in his life her death hadn't really touched him. It hurt Amalie to realize this, but in a way the same could be said of her. Her grief over her sister's death wasn't as strong now as it would have been eleven years ago. Time and distance had come between them, and while it had always seemed Helena was the one building the walls, now Amalie wondered if she herself couldn't have done more to keep in touch.

At the ski store they were fitted with cross-country skis, boots and poles, and Amalie negotiated a special weekly rate. Then they drove the forty minutes back along the Trans-Canada Highway to the information center, where they were given pamphlets describing some of the easier, safer trails they could try.

After pocketing the information, Davin insisted they cross the highway to the Glacier Park warden's office.

"I have to start my research sometime."

"I guess that's true."

The office was on the second story of a low brick compound. There was no formal reception area, just a long narrow corridor, with a number of rooms off it. They found Grant at his desk, in front of a computer screen. Today he was wearing jeans with his standard blue shirt.

"We were just at the information center, looking for a nice safe cross-country skiing route for tomorrow," Amalie explained.

She was relieved that far from appearing annoyed, Grant was obviously pleased they'd dropped by.

His hair was neater today, she noticed, which

only emphasized the uneven length around his ears. His fresh blue shirt, worn with a white T-shirt underneath, had a neat line of white buttons this time, although again, it hadn't been ironed.

Still, none of these details detracted one iota from his very masculine appeal. In fact, she liked that he obviously didn't fuss over his appearance.

"Whatcha doing?" Davin asked, running up and peering over his shoulder.

"Checking out the weather reports. At our remote stations we rely on computer transmissions to keep abreast of the current conditions. I always review them in the morning before I do the *Backcountry Bulletin,* but sometimes I do an update during the day. Like just now, I had a call from some people who're planning an expedition along the Copperstain Trail, out behind old Bald Mountain. They want to know what kind of weather to expect."

"Where's Copperstain Trail?"

Grant pointed to a dotted line on the topographical map that was pinned to the wall.

Amalie searched for the area that Heidi had told them about. She found Bruins Pass on the northwest side of Cheopps Mountain and gently touched her finger to the place on the map. "What about bears, Grant? Do you have many of them in the mountains?"

"Sure. Both black bears and grizzlies." He noticed her shudder. "They generally avoid humans. Avalanches and rock slides present a much bigger risk, although most backpackers don't seem to realize it."

"Rock slides?" Davin's interest had been captured. "Has anyone died from a rock slide?"

"Mountain climbers are always at risk," Grant explained. "Quite a few years back we had a tragic case. A man and woman were driving along the highway, when some loose rock tumbled down from the mountain. One piece broke through the car window, struck the woman on the head. And yes, Davin, she died."

"What are the odds..." Amalie was stunned to think how an accident like that could happen.

"It was a freak event." Grant's tone was meant to reassure.

But the underlying point, it seemed to Amalie, was that there was danger everywhere in these mountains.

"Have you cross-country-skied before?" Grant asked.

"No. We've only gone downhill. We plan to stick to the shorter, level trails around town."

"To start out with," Davin interjected.

Amalie raised her eyebrows. "You say that after the story Mrs. Eitelbach just told us?"

Grant tapped a few keys on the computer, and the screen went blank. "What story was that?"

"It was about a backcountry skiing accident that happened in 1993—"

"One guy died," Davin said excitedly. "The other guy tried to save him, but he was too late. My aunt says I can do a report on avalanches for school, instead of on China. Will you help me?"

This came out in such a rush Amalie was surprised Grant followed any of it.

"I remember that accident all too well. A couple of our men were on the scene within a few hours."

To pull out the dead body. He didn't have to finish his sentence for Amalie to know what had happened. She thought of Helena. And Ramsey. And wondered how Grant could stand it.

"As for your project, Davin, it sounds real interesting. And you're sure in the right place if you want to learn about avalanches. I've got this pamphlet you ought to start with."

He pulled a soft-covered booklet from a desk drawer. On the front was a photograph of a section of the Trans-Canada Highway that looked covered in blockages from avalanched snow. Closer observation revealed strategically placed wooden sheds beneath that snow. The man-made tunnels allowed traffic to travel freely, unimpeded by the heavy drifts overhead.

"Wow! Are these the tunnels we drove through coming from Calgary?"

"Not tunnels. Snow sheds."

"Snow sheds. Right."

"You can borrow this," Grant said, passing it to the boy. "Use one of the empty desks in the next room if you want to get started right away."

"Sweet!" Davin left the room, his head already tucked between the pages.

Amalie watched in wonder. "I haven't seen him so excited by a book in his life."

"Maybe he's caught the bug. This place can be addictive, you know."

"Are you serious?" Obviously some people, Grant included, were happy here. She couldn't understand it. The desolate landscape, bleak weather and isolated location were hardly inviting.

What was it Grant found so appealing? Was it the challenge of his job? "Grant, have *you* ever had to haul dead bodies off these mountains?"

"Yes," he admitted. "But we pride ourselves on the safety record in this park. Over the years we've had very few fatalities, especially along the highway and train tracks."

As if pulled by the mighty mountain peaks outside, Amalie went to the window and stared at the awesome structures. "I guess my sister was one of the unlucky ones."

"Yes. She *and Ramsey* were unlucky. But bad luck was only one ingredient. Poor judgment was the main culprit."

Amalie turned from the mountain view and

thought about what he'd just said. "Why was the accident their fault?"

Grant came up beside her and leaned against the windowsill. "Avalanche conditions were rated high to extreme—Helen and Ramsey had no business on that mountain. A warm spell at the beginning of the week was followed by a heavy blizzard. Any abrupt change in temperature can affect the stability of a weak layer in the snowpack. The added pressure of new snow only increases the risk. Ramsey knew all this."

"But Helena wouldn't have necessarily."

He conceded that point. "Their major mistake, however, was the route they chose. If they'd stuck to the high ridge, they would probably have been okay. Skiing into the steep bowl was suicide."

Amalie moved to the map on the wall, tracing a finger along the Asulkan Brook. She was beginning to know the route well, at least on paper. Grant leaned in from behind her and guided her finger with his hand.

"Here's the hut where they stayed the night. And this is the Pterodactyl."

He released her finger, but she could still feel him behind her, his chest brushing the back of her shoulders. The heat from that one point of contact ran down her body like a shock wave.

"You think Helena skied off the ridge onto the Pterodactyl first?"

His voice came quietly but confidently from behind her. "I know she did."

Amalie took a moment to assimilate this latest revelation, before twisting to face him. "So you blame Helena for the avalanche, and...and for Ramsey's death."

"I guess I do."

It was so unfair! "But you just admitted that Ramsey had the knowledge to recognize the avalanche danger. Not Helena."

"He would have warned her away from that bowl."

"You can't know that."

Their gazes clashed and held. She thought she should hate him for taking such a hard line with respect to her sister.

But she couldn't. He was being honest with her, even if he was mistaken, and that was something she valued. "This is the other reason you didn't like my sister."

"Yes." After a few seconds, the hard line of his mouth softened, and she glimpsed the expression he'd worn last night as they were standing by the door.

"But I like *you*, Amalie," he surprised her by saying. "In fact," he added, "I think I'm starting to like you too much."

CHAPTER SIX

AMALIE STEPPED OUT OF THE SHOWER, remembering the last occasion she'd gone on a date. It had been at least six months ago. The man—a newly divorced X-ray technician—had been introduced by mutual friends, but his reaction to Davin when he arrived to pick her up had ensured that the first date would also be the last.

He hadn't known she had a son.

But Grant did.

Of course, her date with Grant wasn't really a *date*. He was just taking her to the bar so she could find out more about her sister. As she thought about the outing from that angle, Amalie's anticipation did a nosedive into anxiety.

What would she discover about her sister tonight? From all accounts, she couldn't expect to hear anything good. But at least she'd have a few more pieces of the puzzle.

And she would be with Grant Thorlow....

Amalie stood at the mirror, blow-drying her hair. All afternoon, his parting words had stuck with her.

What had he meant when he said he was starting to like her too much?

It was as if he *resented* liking her, as if he'd *expected* he wouldn't. Because of Helena, she supposed.

The real puzzler, of course, wasn't why Grant seemed to like *her*, but how she could be attracted to *him*. He was being so totally unfair where Helena was concerned. About the avalanche, and about Ramsey, too. Ramsey had been the married one; why should Helena shoulder the blame for their affair?

Amalie crossed the hall to her bedroom, slipped into her jeans, then tugged a black sweater over her head. Last summer, before the X-ray technician, she'd gone to a party with a man her friends at work had set her up with. He'd called a couple of times after the party, but each time she'd been busy.

Wasn't she always? Work at the hospital and Davin kept her weeks full. Then most weekends she and Davin were out of town visiting her parents. Where was she supposed to squeeze in a date with that schedule?

Face it, her life had turned out exactly as her mother had predicted: *"If you adopt that boy, you'll never find a husband, never have a family of your own."*

Amalie sectioned off a piece of her fine hair and began French braiding. As long as she lived she'd never understand their attitude. Although he was their own flesh and blood, they'd pushed hard for an outside adoption.

Usually Amalie fell in with their decisions, preferring to keep the peace in the family. But this had been too important. Davin was family; he belonged to them. And so she'd defied her parents, expecting that eventually they'd come to see that she'd been right.

So far, though, it hadn't happened. Oh, outwardly they accepted Davin just fine. But they showed him no warmth, no special care. Of course her parents by nature weren't very affectionate people.

With an elastic, she finished off her hair, then did her makeup. When she surveyed herself in the mirror, it was as if Helena looked back at her. *Don't believe them, Amalie. They just don't understand.*

Amalie blinked, put a hand to her forehead. She hated to admit it, but she was losing faith with her own sister. And it wasn't right. Helena was dead. If she didn't defend her, who would?

A knock at the front door shot Amalie's pulse rate skyward. She pulled off the small plastic stopper on a trial size of her favorite perfume and dabbed scent against her wrists, behind her ears. Carefully she replaced the stopper and went to the door.

Grant filled the entryway. No man she'd ever known, let alone dated, could come close to him in terms of masculinity or strength. Although he was sometimes outspoken and awkward with words, he had the kind of physical assurance that came from having pitted himself against one of the strongest forces of nature—and won.

The idea that this man could be somehow fighting an attraction for her was suddenly ridiculous.

"You're out of uniform," she said, realizing he wasn't wearing his standard light-blue shirt. Instead, he had on a leather coat, which he wore open, revealing a black corduroy shirt buttoned over a black T-shirt. Formfitting jeans tapered at his waist and bulged at his thighs. Dark blue and stiff, they must have been new.

"I guess I am." He was looking at her, as if her black sweater and jeans were somehow special. She noticed a scattering of droplets on his shoulder. "Still snowing?"

He nodded. "Perfectly formed little stellars."

"Huh?"

"Those pretty star-shaped snowflakes. You know, the kind you cut out of paper as a kid."

"Don't all snowflakes look like that?"

"Depends on the temperature. If it was warmer outside we'd be seeing more of a needle-shaped crystal formation."

Grant scanned the room. "So where's Davin?"

"He's over at Heidi's for the night."

"Heidi's?" Grant pulled back a step. "You've got to be kidding."

"Amazing, isn't it?" Amalie grabbed her jacket, locked the door behind her and followed Grant to his truck, explaining as they walked.

"They seem to have taken a shine to each other. Davin was fascinated by that story she told us. When I asked Heidi if she knew of any baby-sitters, she offered to have him herself. She'll probably fill his head with more details of gruesome backcountry avalanche accidents."

Grant laughed. "He sure has the bug, doesn't he?"

"Yes..." Amalie wasn't sure she approved. The last thing she wanted for Davin was a career as dangerous as Grant's.

Not that it was very likely. At age three Davin had been equally obsessed with firefighters. But that had passed. So, in a couple of years he'd probably have a new fascination. Hopefully, by the time he reached college age, it would be for something practical like law or accounting. Practical and *safe*.

THE ROCK SLIDE SALOON was busy this Friday night. As Amalie had expected, most of the people were wearing jeans and drinking beer, and the music that pulsed from the cheap sound system was pure country.

"Let's start with the bartender," Grant suggested, using his shoulder to break a path through the crowd.

Amalie felt as if everyone in the room watched her make her way to the bar. Open stares, covert glances and a localized hush marked her slow progress to the tall wooden counter, where a balding man, probably in his forties, was passing out glasses of beer.

"Toby!" Grant raised his voice to be heard above the din.

"Hey, Thorlow." The bartender answered casually, until he glanced up and noticed Amalie. Then he whistled.

"Man. I heard you were the spitting image, but this is incredible."

Amalie felt like an item on auction as he came out from behind the bar and walked around her. He whistled again, then held out his hand. It was soft, warm and sweaty and she pulled her own back quickly.

"Toby Ward," he said, introducing himself. "You aren't here looking for a job, are you?"

Amalie smiled uncertainly. Was the man kidding? It appeared he was, as he slapped her on the back.

"Boy, do we miss your sister. Bad break about the accident. Must have been a bit of a shock, hey?"

Amalie blinked as she realized these clumsy

words were the first gestures of true sympathy she'd received since she'd arrived in Revelstoke.

"Yeah, your sister was quite the woman." Toby clapped her on the back one more time before returning behind the bar. "First drink is on me. What'll it be?"

They both ordered draft beer, and while they waited for Toby to fill glasses, Amalie wondered what "quite the woman" actually meant.

"Sexiest lady this side of the Pacific Ocean." Toby clarified as he passed them their drinks, obviously checking how well Amalie filled out her sweater at the same time.

Grant moved closer to Amalie, positioning one shoulder to block Toby's view. "Amalie hadn't seen her sister in a while. She was kind of curious to talk to some of her friends...."

Toby propped an elbow on the bar. "Sure thing. What do you want to know, beautiful?"

It was hard to know where to start. "Did she ever confide in you? Tell you what she was doing here or what her plans were?"

Toby laughed. "Her plans, as far as I could tell, were to have a good time. Sometimes she drank a little on the job. I could've nailed her for that, but hey, I'm no fool. That woman drew in customers."

"When did Helena start waitressing for you?"

"What'd you call her? Helena?" Toby shrugged. "She went by plain Helen around here. And she applied for the job the very day she arrived in town. She came into the bar with the ranger who'd stopped her at the gas station. That would be Ralph Carlson, sitting right there, in the corner.''

Toby jerked his head to the left, and Amalie turned accordingly, recognizing the man immediately. Grant had introduced them the first day she'd arrived at Rogers Pass.

"Anyway," Toby was wound up and needed no prompting, "I had one of those cardboard signs, Help Wanted, you know the kind, and she picked it out from the window and put it on the counter, just as plucky as could be. 'What kind of help?' she asked, and damn, if she didn't have a voice just like Kathleen Turner's in *Body Heat*. Kind of husky, you know, only with a trace of an accent...like yours. I hired her on the spot.''

Finally, she'd met someone who actually admired her sister. Too bad the qualities he appeared most drawn to were so superficial. He didn't seem to have known the *real* Helena.

"What about after-hours?" she asked. "Did my sister have any other friends she spent time with?''

Toby's pale-brown eyebrows pushed up against the creases of his forehead. "After-hours was party time. Right, Clinton?''

An older man with yellow hair and a grizzled face had just stepped up to the bar. He nodded at

Toby, then turned his head sideways to give her an assessing look.

"Hard to believe there were *two* of you." He slapped the counter and placed his order. "Gimme a Natural Blonde, would you, Toby?"

At Amalie's double take, he shrugged and held up his hands. "What? It's a beer. Trust me."

She had to read the label to believe him. Sure enough, it was brewed by Wild Horse in Penticton.

"How about another draft for the lady?" Clinton asked.

Amalie shook her head, holding up her full glass. "This will be fine. Thanks, anyway."

"Not so much like your sister after all," was the newcomer's comment.

"I was just telling the lady about those parties Helen used to have." Toby popped the top off a brown bottle and slid it across the counter.

Clinton caught it and raised it to his mouth, tipping his head back and guzzling lustfully.

Oh, no. Amalie didn't think she wanted to hear about the parties that had annoyed Heidi so much.

She turned to Grant, her shoulder bumping into his chest. "I can't take this..."

"There's room at Ralph's table," he said, speaking inches from her ear. "Want to sit down?"

"Yes." She followed him gratefully, leaving Clinton and Toby reminiscing about some of Helena's more memorable antics.

"Hey, Ralph. Mind if we join you?"

Ralph half raised himself from his chair, waiting until Amalie was sitting, before lowering his back-side again.

"I'm sorry," Amalie said to Grant once they were seated. "I'd hoped for so much more. They made my sister sound like some sort of bimbo."

Grant said nothing, obviously too polite to remind her that he'd warned her she'd hear things she wouldn't like.

She lifted her glass and pushed at the cardboard coaster left behind, noting the soft, tacky feel of the finish on the pine table.

"How *did* Helena end up in Revelstoke?" she asked Ralph.

The ranger was no longer wearing his forest-green Parks Canada uniform but was dressed in jeans and a plaid cowboy shirt. The beers he'd consumed up to this point had obviously relaxed him.

"I spotted your sister at the PetroCan gas station off the Trans-Canada. She was driving east, and the snow was really coming down. I took one look at her little Mercedes coupe with summer-tread tires and knew she'd never make it. I told her she'd better get herself a set of all-season radials if she planned to do any more traveling this winter."

"What did she say?"

"She said she couldn't afford new tires."

"What about chains on her tires, instead?" Grant asked.

"I suggested those, too, but she said she wasn't sure. Anyway—" Ralph stroked his mustache carefully, as if surprised to find it on his face "—I was just coming off duty, and asked her if she wanted any coffee. She said she'd rather have a beer. We ended up here." At this point, Ralph pulled at the collar of his shirt.

Right away Amalie realized what had happened. The ranger had tried to hit on her sister! Grant, smirking into his beer, had obviously come to the same conclusion.

"It was the strangest thing. One minute I was offering to help install chains on her car, then she got up to visit the restroom, and the next thing she was telling Toby she wanted the job advertised in his window."

"When was that, Ralph? Do you remember?" she asked.

"A few weeks before Christmas, I think."

Yes. It had been mid-December, and Amalie had been at a meeting at work, when she'd felt the most dreadful, sinking feeling. Unable to explain the sensation at the time, she'd just pushed it out of her mind. Now she was almost positive something bad had happened to Helena. Something that had sent her fleeing from her life in Seattle.

"Did my sister tell you anything about where she was coming from?"

Ralph shook his head. "Once she'd asked about the job, she was full of questions. Where to find an apartment, how to go about selling her car...."

"What did you tell her?"

"Well, I said put an ad in the paper. And it worked, too, although I don't imagine she got much for a vehicle like that in a place like this. Especially in winter."

"I wonder where was she headed." Amalie wished she could figure it out. Somehow it seemed important. She wanted to believe that Helena had been coming home, to see her and Davin.

If only she'd stuck to her plans and made it. Fixed the tires, persevered with the journey. Maybe they'd be together right now, instead of separated forever.

But wasn't that so like her sister? For once, what she was hearing about Helena felt right. The smallest problem had always had the ability to knock her off course.

"Well, that's it for me, I think." Ralph pushed his empty beer bottle to the center of the table, then nodded farewell.

Amalie watched him leave, suddenly tired and discouraged. Grant was right; she shouldn't have come. Clearly, Helena hadn't confided in any of these people.

But she had to have trusted *someone*. She'd lived here almost two months.

Ramsey. Of course it would've been him. Helena's one true friend was Ramsey Carter, but he couldn't help Amalie understand what was happening in her sister's life because he, too, was dead.

Oh, it was all such a mess.

Grant reached out, offering comfort with his touch. "I wish it had worked out differently for her, for the both of you."

A gentle ballad began playing in the smoky bar. The way Gordon Lightfoot sang about reading his lover's mind reminded Amalie of the way she'd once been able to read Helena's.

The sudden shift from fast-paced, raunchy country tunes seemed to catch everyone off guard. The room quietened; the low lighting became dimmer.

"Dance?" Grant was standing, holding out his hand.

Since moving out of her parents' home, Amalie had danced at a few of her friends' weddings and gone to a local club a couple of times. But she still wasn't very confident. "I'm not that good..."

"I don't really care." He took her hand and led her to the dance floor. Once there, he placed his other hand at the small of her back. Now they were standing so close just the merest sliver of air separated them.

Turning her face, she could see the curve of his

ear, the strong line of his jaw, the windblown
bronze of his skin. In the places where her hands
rested—on his shoulder and around his waist—she
felt dense muscle mass beneath soft textured corduroy.

The music flowed in waves of longing around
them. With Grant's arms to guide her, following his
movements was easy. Once she forgot about her
nervousness, Amalie realized that Grant was singing. She could just make out his voice, layered over
the recorded music, low-timbered and perfectly on
key. It seemed natural to close her eyes, and to let
him lead her slowly, smoothly, around the perim-
eter of the small dance floor.

Other couples were dancing, too. Occasionally
she felt their bodies brush past, or heard the murmur
of their voices, but Grant kept her safe in the for-
tress of his arms, crooning words in her ear that
transported her out of this town, to a place that for-
merly existed only in her imagination.

Something powerful welled up inside her; it was
like magic, lifting her feet from the ground and fill-
ing her head with the most exciting anticipation.

This was *it,* she realized. That special something
that she'd always thought people exaggerated, because she'd never felt it once, not on any of her
handful of assorted dates. Those men had held her
hand, danced with her, kissed her good-night and
never had she felt this euphoric pleasure.

Halfway through the song, Grant pulled her closer. Now she felt his chest, his thighs, the metal clasp of his belt. Vague desires became more specific, and she thought in terms of a physical need that she rarely acknowledged.

I want... I want...

She'd been a mother before she'd had the opportunity to lose her virginity. She'd gone from living at home under strict rules to trying to provide a stable home for a helpless infant.

Now she knew those were only excuses for why romance had never swept her off her feet.

The truth was, she'd never met anyone like Grant Thorlow before.

Lifting her head slightly, she brushed her face against his neck, loving the feel and the scent of the man. He responded by tightening his arms and drawing in a breath that expanded his chest into hers.

His opinion about Helena aside, all her instincts told her this was a decent, honest man. Strong and brave, the kind of guy a woman ran to when she needed help.

What really drew her, though, was the way he made her feel when he looked at her. Not like a mother or a daughter, a friend or a sister. And not a good-looking babe he'd like to lure to his bed and forget the next day.

Grant Thorlow made her feel like a desirable, lovable woman.

Amalie wished the song would never end, but of course it did. Within a single beat, a new tune began playing, a raunchy line-dancing song that would have everyone in the room linking arms and do-si-doing.

For a moment she sagged against Grant's chest. Grant seemed equally reluctant to let her out of his arms. "I hate this song, but I'll put up with it if you stay here with me."

"We can't, Grant. We'll be trampled." Already lines were forming, edging them off the small dance floor.

Grant kept his hand at her back as they maneuvered past tables. Just as she was about to turn and sit down, Amalie noticed a man staring at her from a few tables over.

He sat alone, with two glasses—one empty, one half-full. Probably in his midthirties, he had something anxious, almost desperate in his expression, which gave her the shivers.

When he saw that he'd caught her attention, he raised his glass in a silent toast. Then his gaze drifted to Grant and he shook his head as if to show his disappointment in seeing them together.

"Do you know that man over there?" she asked Grant several minutes later. "Sitting by himself, wearing the white shirt and tie."

Grant cast his eyes over the crowd until he saw who she was talking about. "No," he said. "He doesn't look familiar. Why?"

"He was watching me earlier. As though he knew me." More likely, he'd thought she was Helena. But surely everyone in town had heard of the accident and knew Helena was dead.

Grant was obviously thinking along the same lines. "Maybe he was struck by the resemblance."

"That must have been it." And yet she'd had the definite impression he was trying to communicate with her.

"IT'S AFTER MIDNIGHT. I had no idea it was so late." Amalie checked her watch while Grant opened the apartment door for her.

"Should I go down to Heidi's and get Davin for you?"

"No, he's staying the night." Their glances connected, and the longing she'd felt on the dance floor suddenly returned.

"Right." Grant nodded, broke off eye contact. "You did say that. I'd forgotten."

"Coffee?" she asked, tilting her head toward the open door.

"Yeah." He cleared his throat. "Yes, that would be nice."

Too bad Helena's apartment made for such a dismal setting. They avoided the stark living room and ended up sitting at the kitchen table, waiting for the coffee machine to do its thing.

"Thanks for taking me, Grant, and introducing me to those people."

"I'm sorry you didn't find what you were looking for."

Amalie nodded. "Maybe you were right. Maybe it was a mistake that I came out here."

A loud gurgle from the machine on the counter signaled that the coffee was ready. They stood at the same time, with Grant reaching for the mugs while she pulled a carton of milk from the fridge. In front of the coffee machine, they both stopped. Grant put the mugs on the counter, then took the milk from her hands.

"You've been disillusioned," Grant said, laying his hands on her shoulders.

At his touch, Amalie's heart began a steady hammering against the wall of her chest. "I thought Davin should know the truth about his mother. Now I'm not so sure...."

"Will you be going back to Toronto?"

Amalie considered the idea for only a moment. "Not yet. I don't feel right about leaving until Helena's body is recovered. We've come this far—we might as well see it through to the end."

Grant still had his hands on her shoulders. Now she slipped hers around his waist and rested them lightly on the waistband of his jeans. She examined his face, gauging his reaction. "Disappointed you're not getting rid of us?"

"Hardly." His chest expanded on a full breath of air, and his head lowered a few inches.

The mouth that had sung love songs next to her ear earlier was slowly moving toward her lips. The possibilities she'd imagined on the dance floor now seemed entirely within reach. So badly she wanted this man's touch, his warmth...

And yet, she was afraid.

"Grant, I—"

Then his lips were on hers, erasing the words she'd been struggling to find.

CHAPTER SEVEN

GRANT HAD NEVER COMPARED one woman's kiss with another's, but if he'd tried with Amalie Fremont, he would've failed. When his mouth found hers, tentative yet willing, he knew he'd never experienced anything like it before.

On the dance floor he'd felt such an overwhelming longing. Not just a sexual response, but an aching need that reminded him of how alone he'd been these past few years. Amalie in his arms was so fragile and light. He'd wanted to shield her from the ugly truth about her sister; no, he'd wanted to make her *forget* about her sister, to think about him. Only him. The way he'd been constantly thinking of her from the moment they'd met…

She was so beautiful. He still found it odd that her identical twin sister had never evoked the same response in him. Which only proved this wasn't just a physical thing. But he'd already known that. Amalie intrigued him. She was intelligent and strong, yet had this appealing naive side she tried so hard to hide.

He wanted to explore all aspects of this woman.

And yes, he wanted to make love to her. The way she yielded in his arms, she wanted the same thing. That ought to make the situation simple, but he knew it wasn't. The wrong move on his part could send her running.

Still, to hold back was hard. His body was trying to call the shots: *Run your hands over the curves of her hips. Pull her closer. Let her know how much you want her.*

But all his delicious impulses were thwarted when he considered the emotional angles. Was his desire truly reciprocated? Or was he taking advantage of a woman who was still distraught over the loss of her sister?

He hadn't been very kind about Helen's death. He felt sorry about that, now that he knew Amalie better. Even Toby at the bar had managed to come up with more words of sympathy, in a brief meeting, than he himself had managed over several days.

Exercising great restraint, he softened his kisses, while stroking her bound hair with one hand. If only he could go back to their first encounter and play it all out differently this time.

"Amalie." Her name was like music to him, as potent as the love ballad they'd danced to earlier. He kissed her again, gently taking her head between his hands and allowing his mouth to touch lightly over her cheeks, her brow, the small curve of her nose.

When he paused, Amalie opened her eyes and stared at him. "This doesn't make any sense," she whispered.

"Don't say that."

"Not even if it's true?"

Disappointment settled his feet firmly on the kitchen floor. He became aware of his own heavy breathing, the smell of coffee in the air, the knocking from the radiator against the wall.

"I didn't anticipate this development," she said.

"Believe me, neither did I." He'd thought he would hate Helen's sister. How wrong he'd been.

"Grant, you need to understand something. About me. About tonight..."

That was just it, he thought to himself. He already felt he understood. There was something about this woman that he recognized in himself. That was part of the attraction, the pull....

But Amalie was slipping from his arms. He felt a rush of cold air as she left.

"This is happening too fast," Amalie said. "No matter what you might have thought about Helena, I'm not—"

"I stopped comparing you with your sister the second day I knew you," he said.

"Then what are we doing?"

"We *were* kissing."

"Yes. And we both know where that was heading. Look, Grant, I'm only here for a short while. It would be wrong for us to become involved...."

Grant couldn't listen. He stood mutely, helpless against her objections, knowing that the right words were out there somewhere, if only he could find them. The words that would make her understand how he felt when he looked at her, when she was pulled tight in his arms.

Hell. He'd blown it. He unhooked his coat from the kitchen chair, shrugged it onto his shoulders. "I'm sorry, Amalie. I never meant to offend you."

"Oh, Grant." She reached out a hand, trailed it down his sleeve. "I'm just not the sort of woman who gets involved in casual affairs."

"Unlike your sister." That was below the belt. He was sorry the second the words were out. "I apologize for that. I hear what you're saying. I guess I'm just disappointed."

"So am I," she said softly, which confused the hell of out him. If she was sorry, then why...?

Bloody hell. He zipped up his jacket. Nothing she said made sense, at least not to him. Did all men have this much trouble comprehending the opposite sex? On his way to the door, he remembered promising Davin he'd give them cross-country skiing lessons. "About tomorrow..." he began.

"I'll explain you couldn't make it."

That surprised him. "I'd rather not let him down."

"Oh."

"I'm happy to give Davin lessons, Amalie. You, too, if you're okay with it."

"I've never been on cross-country skis before. Neither has Davin."

"Hey, I'm up for the challenge."

"I only hope I am."

"You will be." He glanced at the door, then back to the woman. Now he was sure he saw regret in her eyes. He wished the night could have ended differently. Wished he could understand if the fault had been his or just the circumstances.

"If I got a little carried away tonight, well, I'm sorry about that."

"You don't have to be sorry, Grant. I'm not."

He stepped out into the hall, then turned back for a final glance. Wisps of blond hair were trailing from her braid, her cheeks were pink, her eyes so blue... God help him, how could he leave?

"Just so you know," he said. "My feelings for you...they're definitely not casual."

He didn't wait to see her reaction to that. Just headed for the stairs, treading lightly so as not to disturb the other tenants. He'd go home now and fall into bed, but he knew he wouldn't sleep.

And he'd thought Helena was the dangerous one.

AMALIE SPENT THE NIGHT thinking of Grant's kisses and the way she'd felt dancing in his arms. Around three in the morning, she began to wonder if she'd made a big mistake turning him away.

True, the timing was rotten and the possibilities for their romance to go anywhere seemed limited, but Grant was special. She wasn't likely to run into someone like him in the hospital corridors of St. Mike's, or in the frozen food section of Loblaws.

So why not grasp the opportunity while she had it?

Somehow her youth had passed, now she was approaching thirty without ever having truly fallen in love. Not that she wasn't happy. She loved Davin and never regretted her decision to raise him herself. Her job had its rewards and she enjoyed it; she had lots of friends.

It was just that in Grant's arms she was reminded of the things she'd missed out on.

Romance and love. Marriage and a child, a brother or sister for Davin.

The next day, after coffee and toast, Amalie prepared for the planned skiing expedition. She hiked the rental skis on her shoulders and went outside to the car. For the first time since they'd arrived, it was neither snowing nor cloudy. For a moment she paused, admiring the jutting snow-capped mountains against the backdrop of an aquamarine sky. It was beautiful, she had to admit.

She laid the skis out on the roof rack of the Jetta and, with a length of cord, tied them securely, doubling over several times to make sure the knots would hold. The noise of a loud engine caught her attention and she glanced up to see a dirty white van pull out from the opposite side of the street.

The van moved forward a few yards and stopped in front of her. Then the driver rolled down his window. It was the guy from the bar. The one who'd been watching her so intensely. He appeared younger in the light of day, about her age, and quite unsure of himself.

Just as he was about to speak, Heidi came out of the apartment wearing a red sweatsuit, with Mickey Mouse on the front. The same suede slippers were on her feet, and once more her hair was in curlers. Amalie wondered when she was planning to take them out.

"Davin's still finishing his pancakes," Heidi said. "Come in, I've made one for you."

The man rolled up his window and drove off. Amalie gave the rope one final tug; it seemed secure to her.

"Thanks, Heidi, but I've already eaten." She followed her landlady to the main-floor apartment. "I hope Davin wasn't any trouble last night."

"We watched horror movies until midnight." Heidi sounded smug.

Inwardly, Amalie groaned.

"Then had a hot toddy and went to bed." Heidi caught Amalie's stricken look and laughed. "Didn't put any rum in Davin's. But there was plenty in mine."

She paused at the door to the apartment, before piercing Amalie with another of her scalding looks. "But not so much that I didn't hear you and Grant get home. And him leave a half hour after that."

Amalie didn't know whether to laugh or blush.

Heidi, as usual, forestalled any reaction. "Only half an hour? Surely the two of you can do better than that."

"NOT TOO EXCITING," Grant said, standing at the beginning of the trail, at the base of Summit Road. "But it's a good place for learning."

Ahead, two tracks had been groomed into the hard-packed snow. Grant had explained that you just put one ski in each track, then pushed forward. Sort of like a slow jog, he'd said, keeping your poles on either side for balance.

It sounded like tough work to Amalie. Plus she was cold. Grant had insisted she leave her heavier coat behind and wear layers instead. So she had on a long-sleeved T-shirt with a sweater and a windbreaker over that. But she still shivered in the stiff breeze.

The happy grin on Davin's face made it all worthwhile, though. He'd slipped on his boots and snapped them into the skis as if he'd been doing this all his life. Now he stood just up ahead, stamping his feet impatiently.

"Can we get going?"

After three kilometers, Amalie was glad she'd taken Grant's advice about her coat. She'd already peeled away her windbreaker and stuffed it into the pack on her back, and *still* she was hot.

As she approached Grant, who'd stopped to wait for her, she allowed herself a small complaint. "This is harder than it looks."

She'd been passed by several more experienced skiers, who'd glided past her in a few effortless strokes.

"What am I doing wrong?" Davin was so far ahead he was out of sight. Grant kept skiing back and forth between the two of them.

"You're doing great for a beginner. Hang in there, we're more than halfway. This trail loops back to where we parked our cars."

"Ohhh." She planted her poles in front of her and leaned her weight on them. "Can't we stop for a break? Where's Davin?"

"Just a little farther on. We can rest for ten minutes, then I'll run ahead and catch him."

"Easy for you to say." And do. Amalie envied the excellent conditioning that made this outing little more than a walk around the block to him.

And he looked so good, too, which was doubly

unfair. His blue GoreTex ski pants and jacket clung to his every well-defined muscle as if to taunt her. *See what you turned away last night?*

Lord, even Heidi thought she was a fool. *Only half an hour? Surely you can do better...*

"I have hot chocolate and trail mix." Grant slung his pack off his shoulders.

"Is that a bribe? If so, I accept." She followed him off the trail to a fallen tree behind a screen of evergreens. Placing her skied feet carefully on either side of the log, she sat down and watched him pour from the thermos.

She accepted the drink and a handful of mixed nuts and dried fruit. "Among the dozens of people who've passed me already were two children who didn't look old enough to walk, and a pregnant woman with a child on her back."

Grant laughed, then settled beside her. After a few seconds of silent regard, he reached up to tug at her pale-blue headband. "You're doing okay. Your balance is good. It's just a question of finding the right rhythm."

Funny how that little touch made her insides glitter, just like snow crystals in sunlight. She remembered him saying his feelings for her weren't casual, and wondered what he'd meant, exactly.

When she was done her cocoa, he took the cup from her and set it on the ground by his pack.

"Thanks, Grant. That was just what I needed."

"Really?"

At the question in his voice, she knew he was right. It wasn't nutritional sustenance that her body required at this moment, but something quite different, something that thrilled her almost as much as it scared her. In the back of her mind, she heard her mother's voice: *No man will want you,* and she thought, *It isn't true!*

Or was it? Grant stood and offered a hand. When she took it, he pulled her up so quickly she almost tumbled into his arms.

"Hey," he said, straightening her with his hands on her waist. "You may not be the best skier out there, but you're definitely the prettiest."

Now she was having trouble catching her breath again and it had nothing to do with skiing. The look in his eyes was reminiscent of last night, only not so intense. If she'd thought she'd scared him off with her parting words, obviously she'd been mistaken.

And right now she was glad of it.

"Grant—"

For one beautiful moment she anticipated his kiss. First she closed her eyes, then leaned slightly forward. Just as she felt the brush of his lips, though, her right foot slid forward, crossing one ski over the other. Grant tightened his hold on her waist as she lost her balance. For a moment she thought he'd saved her. Then his eyes widened, and he fell backward, bringing her right on top of him.

"Ouch!"

"I'm sorry!"

The tangle of skis and poles and limbs resembled an advanced game of pickup sticks. Amalie, whose fall had been nicely broken by Grant's body, started to apologize again, but Grant was laughing too hard to hear her.

"I told you I was hopeless," she said, trying to roll onto the ground so he could get up. She was mortified by her clumsiness. Trust her to spoil one of the most romantic moments of her life. But Grant's arms were still around her waist and he wasn't letting go.

"Grant?"

He wasn't laughing anymore. All at once it was so quiet she could hear them both breathing.

"Are you okay?"

"Not yet," he said. And then he kissed her.

CHAPTER EIGHT

ALTHOUGH SHE DIDN'T COMPLAIN, Grant could see Amalie was tired after their ski. He loaded the equipment on the top of her Jetta for her, then suggested they go out for pizza.

"You're not even breathing hard, are you?" Amalie pulled off her blue headband and her fair hair fell forward. He would have liked to brush it back with his fingers, but Davin was there, kicking out the row of icicles that had formed along the bumper of his truck.

"I've spent half my life on skis," he reminded her. He bent to help her remove her boots. "It takes a while to get in condition."

"Davin doesn't seem tired, either."

Grant glanced over his shoulder. Davin was flashing one of the longer icicles like a sword in the air, leaping from one side to the other as he dueled an imaginary opponent.

"He's a kid. Come on, food is what you need. Follow my truck. The restaurant's on Mackenzie Avenue." He dug his keys out of his pants pocket, then waited while Amalie got Davin settled in the Jetta.

One of his buddies had left Parks Canada a few months ago to open Pizza Paradise, a franchise operation headquartered in Winnipeg. Out of his desire to see his friend succeed, and his own love of pizza, Grant had quickly become a regular.

Once everyone was ready, Grant took off down the road, careful to keep an eye on the Jetta behind him. Despite her complaints, he thought Amalie had caught on to cross-country skiing rather easily. It helped that she had downhill experience. As for Davin, he was a natural on skis. Grant figured the boy would love the challenge of the backcountry— if Amalie could ever be persuaded to let him go.

That he found himself thinking of the future again—when he already knew they didn't have one—worried him. Yes, Amalie was different from her sister. But how different? He didn't want to hurt her or the boy. He didn't want to hurt himself, either.

Last thing he'd expected was to fall for Helen Fremont's sister. But that was exactly what was happening. He knew there were plenty of people in town who'd have a hard time believing it. Most especially Ramsey's wife, Denise. She was still angry about Amalie being in town, and was unwilling to listen to a word he spoke in her defense.

Which reminded him, he'd promised to work on

the Carters' basement tomorrow, and had been invited to stay to dinner afterward. Denise's parents had driven back to Kelowna, and he knew she was lonely. He also knew she wouldn't appreciate him spending so much time with Amalie and Davin. She'd see it as a breach of loyalty, which was ridiculous.

But maybe Denise was entitled to a little leeway. She'd just lost her husband, after all. And Amalie looked so much like the woman who'd been responsible.

Grant slowed and gestured Amalie toward a parking space, then levered his own truck into a spot farther down the block. Blaine Macleod greeted him in the restaurant's foyer.

As usual, Grant did an involuntary double take. Man, but it was strange to see Blaine in a white shirt and tie, instead of his former park uniform. Grant didn't know if he'd ever get used to the change. Or understand it. Why choose to work inside a building when you could be out in the mountains, instead?

"Hey, buddy, good to see you." Blaine's glance slid to Amalie; predictably, his eyes widened.

"How's the pizza business, Blaine? This is Amalie Fremont and her nephew, Davin."

"Welcome to Revelstoke. Sorry about your sister. You sure are the spitting image..." He pulled his eyes back to Grant. "In answer to your question, business is good. Here, let me show you to a booth.''

Blaine clapped a hand on Grant's back. "I tell you, being my own boss is the way to go."

"I'm glad you're enjoying it. Have the guys at the franchise headquarters eased up a bit, then?"

"Nah. They're still sending someone out every three weeks or so to check up on me. But he's spending less time with each visit so that's a good sign."

Blaine chatted with Davin for a few minutes about school. Davin told him about the research project he was doing on avalanches and Blaine said he had a story to tell him.

"I'll catch you later, when it's not so busy." Then he left to greet a new group of customers.

"Seems like a nice guy," Amalie said.

"Sure. We're all nice guys here in Revelstoke."

Amalie smiled, then opened her menu. After a lengthy comparison of likes and dislikes, they settled on a large combination pizza and drinks. Once the order was placed, Blaine came back and asked Davin if he'd like to see the kitchen.

"I'll tell you about one of my adventures on the mountain while we're at it," he said, winking at Amalie and Grant.

As soon as her nephew was out of hearing range, Amalie leaned over the table. "Tell me, how is Denise Carter doing?"

"Honestly? Not that good." Right away, Grant felt bad for burdening Amalie. He could tell she felt responsible for Denise's pain, even though it was her sister's fault.

"Poor woman. She's probably still in shock."

Grant agreed. Ramsey's death still didn't seem real to him; he supposed the adjustment would happen over months.

"Denise and Ramsey were married going on eleven years," he said. "Most of that time, I'd swear they were happy. And from the moment Colin was born, Ramsey was a great father. It seems a damn shame for the memory of all those years to be tarnished by the events of the past few weeks..."

"I wish there were something I could do to help her."

"You're not thinking about leaving town, are you?" Grant reached out to grasp her hand. "I don't want you to go."

"But my being here is making her unhappy, isn't it?"

He couldn't deny that. Unfair as it was, Denise's reaction was understandable, too. But still, he didn't want Amalie and Davin to return to Toronto. He wasn't sure where his attraction for her was headed, but he wanted more time to find out.

"It must be hard," he said, "to have someone

dislike you just because you look like someone else.''

Amalie nodded. ''When we were going to school together, that always happened. Only our friends could tell us apart. The other kids tended to treat us as if we were a single unit.''

''All Denise needs is a chance to get to know you as an individual.''

''Not much chance of that happening. I—I won't be here *that* long.''

''No?'' He squeezed her fingers, mimicking the pressure in his own chest. Her uncertainty fueled his desire to be with her as much as possible in the days remaining to them.

Davin came back from the kitchen at that moment, and Grant released Amalie's hand, then slid over on the bench seat to make room.

''Wow! Blaine was telling me about how he had to rescue an injured skier. He pulled him on a toboggan for about ten kilometers. Have you ever had to do something like that?'' Davin's voice was infused with admiration.

''I have. Part of our job is helping people who get in trouble in the backcountry.''

''Awesome!'' Davin's eyes couldn't have been any bluer and his lips and cheeks were so flushed they looked artificially colored.

He was a nice-looking kid, Grant realized. Well, how couldn't he be, with his strong resemblance to his mot—no, not his mother—his aunt. Grant checked his own thoughts, thinking it was a weird thing to be an aunt when you were an identical twin. Since Amalie had the exact same set of chromosomes as Helen, genetically speaking Amalie *could* have been Davin's mother.

Certainly, emotionally speaking, she was. Her expression was tender and indulgent as she reached across the table to toss Davin's hair.

"You certainly caught on to cross-country skiing quickly," she said. "How am I ever going to keep up with you?"

"It's so much fun—I love it." Davin reached for a slice of garlic toast that the server had just brought to the table. "It must be really sweet up in the mountains. Hey, Grant?"

Grant noticed how quickly Amalie's smile faded at mention of the backcountry. Two vertical lines formed between her brows as she tucked both hands into her lap.

"You have to be real careful when you venture onto the back slopes," Grant said. "Especially right now, conditions are a little treacherous. We've had a lot of snow this month, and there's a warming trend on the way."

"Does that mean you're going to use the howitzer?" Davin bounced up in his seat.

"Probably."

"When?"

"That depends on the snow. But I'd say sometime this week we'll have to close the highway and do a little control work."

"That is so awesome. Can I watch, Grant?"

"I don't know." Generally members of the public were prohibited from the site. A couple of times they'd allowed in cameramen, working on a film. Once, he'd let his parents stand by the gun while he tracked the avalanches in his truck.

"It's probably too dangerous," Amalie said quickly, picking up on his reluctance, or maybe voicing her own concerns.

"But I need to watch—for my research project!"

Amalie's face had gone pale under the pink streaks put there by the sun and wind. "It's out of the question. Right, Grant?"

"Why? Why is it out of the question?"

Grant felt torn. He could make an exception and permit Davin to observe the shoot. But he suspected Amalie was counting on him to say no. Davin was just so enthusiastic, though. He hated to dampen that.

"It's not that dangerous by the guns," he said tentatively.

Amalie shook her head, but Davin was already standing. "Yes! Yes! Please, Aunty, please let me watch."

"If you wanted," Grant suggested to her, "you could come with him. It's really pretty routine stuff, but you'll have to keep out of the way of the workers.''

"What about you?" Davin asked. "Where will you be?"

"I have to be down the mountain so I can assess how much snow was released and whether we need to aim for any more targets."

Amalie's eyes were huge. "You stand in the path of the avalanche?"

"Well, the idea, of course, is to stand a little farther back than that."

It didn't always work out that way, though, because avalanches weren't completely predictable. A few times he'd been in situations where he'd had to scramble out quickly. But he didn't figure Amalie needed to hear about those right now.

Davin's attention was refocused on his aunt. Grant had never seen a dog look more pleading.

"Well... I don't know."

Grant felt bad for having backed her into a corner. He remained silent, even when Davin tried to press him into the argument on his behalf.

"It's your aunt's decision now, Davin."

"Oh, Davin," Amalie said. "What have I done, bringing you to this place?"

"So I can go?"

"No." Amalie looked across the table at Grant. "*We* can go. If you're going to be out there, then so am I." With a shaking hand, she reached for her glass of water. "I can't say I'm looking forward to it, though."

"ANOTHER PIECE OF CAKE, Grant?" Denise Carter asked.

"No, thanks. I'm stuffed. That was a great dinner." He eased down on the living room sofa, uncomfortably aware of the snug fit of the waistband on his pants. He didn't worry about the weight gain being permanent. The week's work ahead of him would take care of that problem.

"Yes, well, there's been no shortage of food around here. Since Ramsey's—accident, neighbors have been dropping by with baking and casseroles...."

Denise had just put the kids to bed; now she added fresh coffee to his mug. The house was so quiet he could hear the splash of liquid against ceramic. He was exhausted after eight hours of labor in the basement and was wondering how quickly he could excuse himself.

Maybe after this cup of coffee.

"I hope Colin didn't make a nuisance of himself today." Denise sat next to him on the sofa, with her own mug of coffee. She crossed her legs toward him, and that was when he noticed that at some point in the day she'd changed into a dress. She was wearing makeup and perfume, too.

"No." He cleared his throat. "Colin was fine. He's actually quite a hand with the tools."

"Well, he used to spend a lot of time building with Ramsay." Her bottom lip trembled, and she paused. When she spoke again, her voice was firm. "I appreciate your help today, Grant, but I want you to do something else for me."

The coffee was hot, but Grant took a big gulp. "You know I will if I can."

"I want you to find out how long Ramsey had been seeing Helen."

Grant's spirits sank. "Denise, are you sure you want to know? Don't you think it would be better—"

"No." Denise cut him off, pushing her hand up against his chest. "I've thought about it and thought about it. I need to learn the whole truth."

Back to Helen again. The one woman Grant would really rather forget about. "I'm not sure if I'll be able to uncover anything. This affair caught all of us by surprise."

"Then maybe it was the first time they were together. If that turns out to be the truth, it'll at least be some comfort to me."

And what if Helen and Ramsey had been running around for weeks or even longer? How would Denise feel then? Grant knew one thing: if that was the case, he didn't want to be the one to tell her.

"You might not like what you find out...,"

Hadn't he issued the same warning to Amalie? Neither woman, however, appeared willing to take his advice.

"It can't be worse than what I've been imagining...." Denise shrank back against the sofa.

He felt beaten. "Okay, Denise. I'll ask around a little."

Her body relaxed. "Thank you, Grant. I can always count on you."

He was glad she felt that way, but wondered if she had any idea how much time he'd been spending with Amalie lately. He'd meant to bring up her name once or twice this evening just to get Denise adjusted to the idea, but every time he'd chickened out. He was sure she'd be hurt, and he didn't want to add more troubles to her load. But he wasn't willing to stop seeing Amalie, either.

"I'm bushed, Denise. Think I'll head for home."

At the door she wrapped her arms around his neck, and he hugged her in return. "Take care of yourself. And the kids."

"I will, Grant. And thanks again."

Outside, the temperature had gone up a few degrees, despite the setting of the sun. That warm front was coming as scheduled. Grant's feet crunched in the snow as he walked to his truck. What would Amalie think of his new assignment? he mused. Somehow he suspected she wouldn't be impressed if she found out.

Funny how his life had become so complicated. Two weeks ago he'd lost his best friend. Now he felt that Denise expected him to fill the void Ramsey's death had left. To top it all off, he'd fallen in love—with the sister of the woman who'd led Ramsey into betrayal.

And he'd thought controlling avalanches was difficult.

DAVIN WAS READING A BOOK for this week's novel study, when Amalie decided it was time to search the apartment to see if she could find any further documentation belonging to Helena.

There weren't many potential hiding places in the small apartment. Amalie was thorough, even checking under the mattress. All she found were bank records from a local branch—the small checking account was almost always perilously close to overdrawn.

There were no personal letters, except a birthday card she'd sent her sister a few years ago; no hidden credit cards or driver's license. How did anyone get by these days without a credit card? True, Helena had been short of money, but so was Amalie and she had several cards. One for gas, one for her favorite discount department store and her Visa.

And what about Helena's driver's license? She must have had one to drive to Revelstoke. Had she destroyed it when she sold her car? That seemed a little drastic.

It was almost, Amalie thought, as though Helena had wanted to make sure no one could trace her to this town.

But that was crazy. It implied that Helena had done something wrong, possibly illegal, that she was on the run.

Amalie wondered about the life Helena had left behind. Surely there were people she cared about who should be informed of her death. In that other world she might have had business that required attending. Perhaps there'd been insurance. A will.

Probably no insurance or will, knowing Helena. Long-range planning had not been her forte. So who would inherit her jewelry? Some of it appeared very expensive.

Likely me, Amalie realized, since Davin wasn't legally Helena's son. The thought made her nervous, and she decided to contact a lawyer back in Toronto. Having just recently revised her own will, she had a card in her wallet. She flipped past her identification until she located the number she needed, then made the call from the phone in Helena's bedroom.

Quickly she apprised the lawyer of the situation and asked if he could try to find out where Helena had lived and whether she had any friends or roommates who should be notified of her death.

When she hung up the phone, she saw Davin standing in the doorway.

"Were you listening?"

"I'm sorry. I couldn't help it. Were you talking about Helen?"

"Helena," she corrected automatically. "I'm trying to find out where your mother lived before she came here. Whether she had any friends who should be told about her accident."

Davin came into the room and stretched out on the bed beside her; he stared up at the ceiling. "When you find out, are we going to go home?"

"I don't know. I was hoping we could stay until the—the bodies were recovered from the mountain."

Davin didn't seem upset by the mention of bodies. "I like it here. I don't want to leave."

"You just enjoy being out of school." She tickled him under the arms and he rolled up like a hedgehog, giggling. She started laughing, too, and soon they were both tumbling over the bed in a mock wrestling match.

"I win," Davin said when he finally had her hands pinned to her side.

Amalie struggled a little, and was surprised at his strength. She *could* have freed herself if she'd really tried, but not as easily as just a year ago.

"'What price, freedom?'" she said, playing along with him.

"You have to make lasagna for dinner."

"No! No!" She twisted fruitlessly. "Anything but lasagna."

Davin giggled again, and his hold loosened. She flipped him over and held his wrists above his head. "Now *you* have to do what I tell you."

"Wh-what?" he asked between giggles.

"Finish reading your chapters for the day."

"Ohhh."

"Sorry, buddy. It's time to hit the books again."

"That's nasty." He sat up slowly and was just about to stand, when suddenly he grabbed a pillow and flung it at her.

"Gotcha!" he said, then raced back to his book in the living room.

Smiling, Amalie grabbed the pillow, punched it a few times to fluff it up, then put it back on the bed. As she did so, a photograph from her wallet caught her eye. The picture—Helena's last school photo before she left home—must have fallen out during the tussle with Davin. It sat half-obscured by the folds of the quilt.

Picking it up, Amalie looked at the photo that could have been of her.

"What were you doing here, Helena? What were you running away from?"

There was, of course, no answer. Amalie wondered if there ever would be.

DAVIN FLOPPED ONTO THE SOFA with the book Grant had lent him about avalanche control in Rogers Pass. He couldn't understand some of the big words, but still the book was way more interesting than the novel his mom wanted him to read.

Mom.

He wondered what Amalie would say if she found out he sometimes thought of her that way, even though, from as early as he could remember, he'd always called her Aunty, not Mom. Which was weird, since she'd adopted him, and raised him, and was the only parent he'd ever had.

He knew that was because of Helena and because Amalie didn't want to hurt her feelings. It wasn't fair. So what if he'd actually come out of Helena's stomach? That didn't make her a mother.

Especially when she hadn't even kept his pictures.

Davin rolled onto his stomach, which was suddenly feeling a little sick. He was reminded of the way he'd always felt when Helena made one of her rare calls home. He'd hated having to talk on the phone to her. Usually his aunt sat beside him, mouthing stuff for him to say.

He was glad they wouldn't be getting those phone calls anymore. But he didn't know if that meant he was glad Helena was dead. It might have been interesting to meet her, just once. He won dered what her eyes would look like when she was watching him.

Davin rolled onto his side, trying to get comfortable. He stared at a picture in his book, not wanting to think about Helena anymore. Part of him thought Amalie should forget about her, too.

But then they'd have to go back to Toronto, and Davin wasn't ready to leave yet.

Gripping his book, he wondered if Amalie would ever let him go skiing in the backcountry. If they could stay until summer, he could try mountain climbing, too.

One day, when he was older, he'd climb to the top of all the mountains he'd been reading about, mountains he was beginning to know by name: Avalanche Mountain, Eagle Peak, Mount Macdonald.

He would be an explorer, just like Major A. B. Rogers, who'd discovered the pass through the Selkirk Mountains. Or a member of the avalanche control team like Grant. Maybe one day he'd actually *be* in an avalanche himself. He wouldn't die like Helena, or that man in the story Mrs. Eitelbach had told him about. No, he'd be brave; he'd keep his head; he'd be a real hero.

Davin closed his eyes and dreamed....

CHAPTER NINE

GRANT PLACED THE HEAVY CUBE of snow carefully on the slanted platform, then tapped the bottom firmly. A fracture formed about halfway through the cube, and the top layer of snow slid smoothly to the ground. He measured the force required for the fracture, then called the result to Peder Forsberg.

Usually Grant had test results radioed to him at the head office. Today he'd decided to come out to the observation site at Mount Fidelity himself and take a look around.

They'd already done a snow profile. Having completed the shear test, all that was left was to take a trial blast on slope number one. He nodded to Peder, who lit a long match, then held it to the fuse. When he was sure it was ignited, Grant tossed the hand-sized bomb down the slope. A few seconds later it blasted, fracturing the snow and sending it tumbling down to the flats below.

"That was a large release—about fifty centimeters," Peder said.

Grant nodded. "No time to lose. Let's close the highway now and get busy." Conditions were prime. Nothing in the world was going to stop an avalanche from occurring. It was his job, however, to control *when* it happened.

As they drove back to the Rogers Pass office compound, Grant thought about his promise to Denise. He hadn't done anything about it so far, but knew he'd eventually have to work past his reluctance and try to get her some answers.

It seemed Peder's thoughts were on a similar wavelength. Staring out the passenger window, he asked, "I wonder when we'll be able to get up to the Pterodactyl and search for those bodies."

"We have to worry about the highway corridor first," Grant cautioned. "I could see stabilizing the area late next week. After that, we might be able to mount a search operation in a couple of days. Assuming we don't get any more snow," he added.

Peder nodded.

Grant pushed up his sunglasses and cleared his throat. "I still can't believe Ramsey went in there."

Peder nodded. "Bloody suicide, it was. Hope she was worth it."

Normally, Grant would have let that comment lie. But today he cleared his throat again and asked a question. "Any idea how long he was seeing her?"

Peder's sideways glance conveyed surprise. "Not too sure. Blaine might know. I heard they had dinner at his restaurant once."

"Really?" Grant was surprised they would have met someplace so public as Pizza Paradise.

"I guess she had a thing for married men." Peder stretched out his long legs and pushed his light-brown hair from his forehead. "She sure wouldn't give me the time of day."

"What?" Grant swung a glance at the youngest member of his team. "You were interested in her?"

"Who wouldn't be? I first saw her at the Rock Slide Saloon. God, but she was something."

"Did you ever go to any of those parties she was so famous for?"

"Oh, sure. She was wild. I've never seen a woman drink like that. After she'd had enough, she'd get up on the kitchen table and dance. God, Grant, you should've seen her." Peder wiped his brow as if just the memory had him sweating.

"What about Ramsey? Was he ever at those parties?"

Peder looked startled. "Hell, no. Can you imagine straitlaced Ramsey turning up for something like that?"

He fell silent, as if suddenly realizing that what "straitlaced" Ramsey *had* turned up for, had been a hell of a lot more wild.

IT WASN'T SNOWING, but howling winds lifted the surface crystals and created a haze like a dust storm. Amalie held a hand up to protect her face while she watched Grant talk to the man from the Canadian Armed Forces.

The 105 mm howitzer was mounted on huge wheels that allowed it to be moved from one firing location to another. Since the machine couldn't be fired by a civilian, every winter a gunnery unit from the army was stationed in Rogers Pass. A member of that unit was currently talking to Grant.

"It looks like a cannon, don't you think?" Davin asked. He aimed the disposable camera that they'd bought at the drugstore yesterday and clicked a photo.

"It *is* big," Amalie agreed, eyeing the powerful gun, which had just been settled onto a secure concrete pad along the edge of the closed highway. The blowing snow was so pervasive and cloud cover so thick and gray she couldn't even make out the shapes of the mountains where the avalanches were to be triggered.

Beside her was one of Grant's team members, an approachable-looking young man named Peder, who spoke with the slight staccato of a Norwegian accent. His job was to maintain radio control with Grant, who would be watching the imminent avalanche from closer range.

"I think we're ready." Grant's authoritative voice traveled across the expanse of clumpy, old snow. He was dressed warmly in his snow pants and anorak, his head covered by a tight black knit cap and his hands in thick gloves. Still, a frost had formed on the faint stubble of an unshaven day's growth, and his cheeks were ruddy with the cold.

"How will they know where to fire?" she heard Davin ask him. "I can hardly see anything."

She'd been wondering the same thing; she moved in to hear the answer.

"We have stakes set up all along the highway." Grant pointed in front of the gun, where a ribbon of red was just visible through the white haze. "We're going to be shooting about thirty targets today. In three hours, it'll all be over."

He left then to drive his truck down the road to where he would position himself on the target slope. Amalie told herself this was all in a day's business to him; there was absolutely no reason for her to feel tense and worried. Bunching her gloved hands in the pockets of her suede coat, she paced restlessly as Davin bombarded Peder with endless questions.

She could see now why Grant had said they'd be safe. The avalanche they would soon be triggering was well out of range of their current location. Not so for Grant. He was planning to stand right at the foot of the avalanche path. What if he miscalculated the quantity of snow that would be released? What if he was swallowed and buried, like Helena and Ramsey?

"Do you ever worry that something might go

wrong?'' she asked Peder, stamping her feet on the hard concrete pad.

"Not really. And you shouldn't, either." His smile was engaging, reassuring. "We're all well trained, and we don't take unnecessary risks. Grant won't let us."

The radio crackled. Grant's voice was coming in from the distance. "Mount target number three."

The men around the gun moved into action. First the bearing number was called out. Then the elevation.

"Okay," Grant said, "load."

Davin snapped another picture as the missile was loaded into the howitzer.

Suddenly, Amalie realized the wind had died and the snow crystals had settled. Now she saw the outline of the mountain before them.

"Let her go!"

"Fire!"

The howitzer blasted; the empty casing fell to the ground. From the mountain came a rumble, like distant thunder.

"Wow!" Davin clicked another picture, then another. Amalie strained to see in the distance. Grant had warned them that not every cannon shot was successful. But it appeared this one was. As they watched, a huge cloud of snow began to form on the opposite peak.

"The shock waves trigger the release of snow,"

Peder explained as the cloud grew bigger and bigger. "Look closely. As the snowpack travels down the mountain it'll gain speed and momentum and set off the snow in the lower regions."

"Does it look larger than you expected?" Amalie swallowed nervously. Not for a second had she forgotten that Grant was standing at the foot of that mountain.

"It's sizable. But don't worry. Grant knows what he's doing."

Amalie nodded, wrapping her arms around her body as she felt a chill unconnected with the weather conditions. She thought of Ramsey, who also should have known what he was doing. Was Grant right? Had it been Helena's carelessness that had cost them their lives?

Amalie stared up at the mountain slope, unable to see a thing other than clouds of tumbling snow. The rumbling sound gave testament to the forces of nature at work. Where was Grant?

She eyed the radio, willing it to pulse to life with his voice. Only when she heard him would she believe he truly was safe.

GRANT WAS HAPPY with the quantity of snow that came off the mountain during the three-hour shoot. It was definitely more than he'd expected, and a couple of times he'd had to do some quick maneuvering to get out of the danger zone. Now he radioed to Peder and told him they could call it a day.

From his truck, he could see the snowplows already at work, clearing the roads. Within the hour the highways would be open and safe for travel.

Arriving at the last gun position, he found Amalie and Davin waiting for him. Amalie looked cold, those same worry lines etched into her forehead. Davin, on the other hand, was exuberant.

"Well? What did you think?" Grant asked.

"Can I work here with you when I grow up?"

Grant's glance cut to Amalie. The lines on her forehead deepened at Davin's question. He threw an arm around the young boy's shoulders. "You'll probably change your mind ten times between now and when you're finally old enough to make your choice."

"No, I won't."

Davin kicked at a clump of snow, then punched a fist into the air. The kid was euphoric after watching the morning shoot. Looked like he had some energy to burn. "Ever tried snowshoeing?" Grant asked him.

Davin straightened, eyes bright. "No. But I'd like to."

"I'll take you out this afternoon—if your aunt agrees."

She was shaking her head. "Aren't you exhausted?"

"Lunch will revive me. How about we head for pizza?"

By going to Pizza Paradise, Grant was hoping he could get a chance to speak privately to his buddy about that story Peder had told him. Of course he'd have to be subtle. He didn't want Amalie knowing he was investigating her sister's relationship with Ramsey for Denise.

He'd started out trying to help Amalie learn about her sister. Now he'd promised Denise that he'd find out how long Helen and Ramsey had been having their affair. The whole situation was becoming so convoluted he was beginning to feel like a double agent.

This kind of stuff was so easy in the movies. In real life, Grant felt like a jerk. He didn't like searching for information behind Amalie's back or hiding his growing friendship with Amalie from Denise.

James Bond, he definitely was not.

Although, he wouldn't mind trying that sky-diving stunt he'd seen in the last movie, and winning the lady over in the end....

AT THE RESTAURANT, Grant sat back and again reflected on how different Amalie was from her sister. Peder had looked at him as if he were crazy for not having been attracted to Helen. But Grant had never been enticed by superficial beauty. So far all his serious relationships had been with women who shared his passion for adventure and the outdoors.

In that respect, Amalie was an exception. She seemed to have an innate fear of the mountains. But Grant was confident she would overcome it. Once this business with Helen and Ramsey was cleared up.

Today, the soft blue of her sweater matched her eyes, and both reminded him of the sky on a frosty winter afternoon. With her hair pulled back in a ponytail, he could see the sweep of her cheekbones, the sloping line of her jaw, and her small, smooth chin. She looked youthful. But not carefree.

Reaching out, he pressed his thumb along the lines that formed between her brows. "It's over, Amalie. Time to stop worrying."

"It's never over, Grant. Once one problem's resolved, there's always another." She frowned, replacing the lines he'd just tried to erase. "I sound like my mother when I say that."

"Are you sorry you came on the shoot?"

Her gaze slid over to Davin, who was working on his third slice of pepperoni and cheese. "How could I be? I've never seen him so excited. Not even at Christmas."

Davin grinned around a mouthful of food.

"I give you full marks for not letting your fear stand in the way of something that was important to Davin. A lot of mothers couldn't be that brave."

"I felt safer than I expected. The hardest part was knowing you—"

She stopped, but the idea that she'd been concerned for his safety was flattering.

"Have you ever been injured doing avalanche control?" she asked.

"My first year I broke my arm. That's about it." He could see the doubt in Amalie's eyes.

"I still feel people aren't meant to live in this part of the world," she said. "Not just because of the avalanches. I mean, think about it. The terrain is practically impassable. It snows almost all the time, and even your summers are measured in weeks rather than months."

"Now, that's not true—"

"That's what I read yesterday when I was helping Davin with his research."

"Did your research tell you how it feels to stand on the Abbott Ridge Trail and look over the sweep of the Asulkan Valley?" Grant wished he had the words to explain how he felt about these mountains, about this rugged country.

But part of him acknowledged the validity of what she was saying. This area of the world *was* both remote and wild. There were reasons the native Indians had never ventured into the Selkirks, why the land was uncharted and unknown when the first explorers came, searching for a railroad route that was to unite the provinces into one country called Canada.

Those same reasons had cost him a relationship or two in the past. Getting involved with Amalie, he could see, would probably take him down that same path. If he was smart, he'd back away now, before he'd invested too many feelings.

Davin put down the glass that had been full of milk and was now empty. "I saw a neat bookstore down the block. I'd like to check it out for my research. Could I?"

Amalie nodded, no doubt pleased with his interest in books, even though the subject was hardly to her liking. "If you find any that seem interesting, I'll see if I can order them at the library."

Once the boy was gone, Grant stretched an arm over the back of the vinyl seat. "So," he said, "is life much better in Toronto, then? Are you a big-city girl at heart?"

"I wouldn't say that. We didn't actually grow up in Toronto. Our parents lived in a small town about two hours north of the city. We had quite a protected childhood, really. The community revolved around the church, and our parents were pretty strict. They kept a very close eye on us."

He could picture her in a smaller place. "Why did you move to Toronto?"

"I went to university there, planning to return to

work in Barrie when I graduated. It's just north of Toronto, and not nearly as big," she explained.

He nodded. "I've heard of it. What happened to your plans?"

"In one word—Davin. If my parents had been more accepting of him, I probably would've moved closer to home when I finished school."

"What was with your parents? Were they upset that Davin was born out of wedlock?"

"That's an understatement. They barely spoke to Helena again after they found out she was pregnant. They also didn't approve when I decided to raise Davin. They felt Helena should have given him up for adoption."

"But he was their grandson."

"I know. Believe me, I've struggled to understand their attitude. I think it stemmed from disappointment. They came to this country so that Helena and I would have every opportunity. To have Helena drop out of school without her grade twelve..."

"But you got your degree. You're a nutritionist, right?"

"Yes. But they'd hoped I would be a doctor."

"Still, you're hardly a failure." To him, her decision to raise Davin was both noble and courageous. He tried to imagine himself at eighteen, taking sole responsibility for an infant. It was a real stretch. "You're one incredible woman. You know that, right?"

Amalie's rueful smile made her look vulnerable, young. "Come on, Grant. Don't make me out as self-sacrificing. Raising Davin has been the most wonderful part of my life."

"And where was Helen during all this?"

At the mention of her sister's name, Amalie seemed to lower an imaginary protective shield between them. "Don't blame her, Grant. My mother was very hard on her, very critical. At that point in her life, Helena's self-esteem was at an all-time low."

Silently, Grant gave thanks for his own mom and dad. Travelers and adventurers, they'd taken a laissez-faire approach to parenting, but he'd always known they loved and approved of him.

"Did Helen drop out of high school because she was pregnant?"

"No. The pregnancy happened later, once she'd moved to Toronto with a girlfriend. She dropped out of school and left home the day after she'd been chosen for the lead role in the high-school musical."

"I don't get it."

"My mother told her she wasn't allowed to perform in the show."

"You're kidding."

"Afraid not. Helena left home the next day. Her

dream was to model, but she ended up working in retail.''

''And *then* got pregnant?''

''Yes.'' Amalie's expression, as she glanced out the window, became pensive. ''Helena never told me who the father was. She said he didn't care about the baby and didn't have the ability to pay any support.''

''That's a sad story.''

''Yes. I often think Helena's life was full of people who let her down. Some of us did it unintentionally.''

He thought about that word *us*.

''You think you let her down? But you raised her son for her....''

Amalie smiled gently. ''That's something Helena did for *me*. Let me raise her child.''

''I still don't see how *you* let her down?''

''I was always the one who caught on the first time, who did things right, who never made our parents angry. How frustrating it must have been for her to feel she had to try to live up to me.''

''You can't honestly blame yourself for not screwing up.''

''Maybe not. Maybe it was our parents who should have made more of an effort to see us as individuals. They always thought, if Amalie can do it, then why not Helena. I guess their rationale was that we were identical twins.''

"Identical twins, but not identical people."

"Exactly." Amalie touched his hand for a moment, then slid out from the booth. "I need to use the washroom. When I get back we should probably leave, if you plan to snowshoe in the light of day."

"Yes." Grant jerked his thoughts from her childhood, back to the present. If Amalie was going to the washroom, then this was his chance. He had to flag down Blaine.

"Hey there, buddy." The former mountaineer caught Grant waving his arm. "Want a refill on that coffee?"

"No, I just wondered if I could, um..." Grant lost his voice for a second and had to clear his throat. "Could I ask you a few questions?"

"Interested in a change of career?"

Grant grinned at the idea of working in a pizza joint. "Confined indoors ten, twelve hours a day? No, thanks."

He gestured Blaine to sit in the seat opposite him. "I wanted to ask you about Ramsey." He twisted in his seat so he could check the door of the women's washroom. It was still closed. "And Helen," he added.

"Ahhh." Blaine leaned back, a knowing gleam in his eyes. "So you've heard they had dinner here?"

"There was a rumor." Grant tapped his fingers

on the smooth table. Prying was not in his nature. But he'd promised Denise… "Is it true?"

"They came here once. Sat over there." He pointed to a small, out-of-the way booth.

Grant nodded. "Can you remember when that was?"

"About a week before the accident. They seemed to be having a pretty intense conversation. At one point Helen was crying."

Blaine's eyes widened as someone approached from behind Grant's right shoulder. Even before he twisted to look, Grant knew it had to be Amalie. Shifting his gaze, he saw that her expression was grim, her posture tight.

So much for being subtle.

CHAPTER TEN

"TIME TO SETTLE THE BILL." Grant reached into his pocket for his wallet, wondering how much of his conversation with Blaine Amalie had heard.

"You paid last time," she said. "It's my turn."

She'd heard enough, he figured, judging by the frost in her voice and eyes. Not that he blamed her for her anger. Damn, but he was a fool. He should have just told Amalie what he was doing.

Out on the street, he discovered Amalie wasn't the type to stew in silence.

"You were talking about my sister, weren't you?" she asked. "Why were you doing it behind my back?"

He saw no option but to come clean. "Denise Carter asked me to find out how long your sister and her husband had been seeing each other."

Amalie did a double take. "You? Why you?"

It was a good question. "I guess because she trusts me, because I was Ramsey's best friend."

For what *that* was worth. He'd been Ramsey's closest buddy, yet he hadn't had any more clue than

Denise about what was going on. The truth was Denise wasn't the only one who felt betrayed.

"And you couldn't say no?"

He wondered how to explain the duty he felt he owed to Ramsey's widow. "I guess I understand how she feels. See, the Asulkan Hut, where Ramsey and Helen...well, you know. That was Denise and Ramsey's special place. He asked her to marry him there."

Would she get it? It seemed that she did.

"Oh, Grant, of course I understand how awful this situation is for Denise. It's just the idea of you asking questions about my sister without me knowing...." She swiped at an icicle that hung from the awning above the restaurant door; they both watched as it shattered on the concrete sidewalk at their feet.

"It still doesn't make sense to me—that Helen was having an affair with a man who was married."

Grant checked the urge to argue. Despite all Amalie had learned about her sister these past few days, she obviously still didn't believe Helen had changed. What would it take to convince her that her sister wasn't the same person she'd been as a child?

Or maybe she was the same person; only, Amalie had never been willing to face up to her flaws.

"Look, Amalie," he said, putting an arm round her back. "Let's just—"

A voice called out from behind him. "Grant!"

Oh, boy. That sounded like... He turned to find Denise helping Chrissy and Colin out of the back seat of the Jeep.

"Go ahead and get us a table," Denise said, urging the children into the restaurant. Grant held the door open for the youngsters, avoiding Denise's glare. Her anger was hot as she turned from Grant, to Amalie, then back to Grant.

"Together *again?* Clearly, there's something going on here that I don't know about."

"There's nothing going on," Amalie said quietly. "I was just about to catch up with Davin at the bookstore. If you still want to take him snowsnoeing," she added, transferring her gaze to Grant, "you'll find us there."

He nodded, then watched her deliberate retreat. Which left him with Denise, who was eyeing him very suspiciously.

"I just don't understand it. After what her sister did to us—"

"Amalie is not Helen," he said, determined to stand his ground. Then Denise put a hand over her eyes, and he saw her shoulders tremble. Compassion kicked in. "I'm sorry, Denise. I *have* been trying to find out about—about what you asked me."

She stilled. Took a deep breath. "And—?"

"A week before the accident they met here for

pizza. Blaine said they seemed to be discussing something serious and Helen was very upset."

Denise's gloved hand went to her forehead. "So they'd been together for a while. It wasn't the first time—"

He'd have liked nothing better than to dispute that, but he'd come to the same conclusion. If Helen had been crying, then something had to have already happened between them. "Maybe Ramsey was trying to call things off."

"Oh, Grant." Denise leaned against him, blotting tears with her leather-covered fingers. "He never should have started anything in the first place."

"I know…" He placed a hand on her shoulder. Beneath the jacket she felt so fragile.

"Ramsey's hours between his practice and the hospital were always crazy. I never called to check up on him or worried about where he was. I just trusted him."

"I know."

"I thought we had a good marriage, that he was happy. The night before he left we made love."

That sounded like a good thing, although Grant was really uncomfortable with such intimate confidences. Withdrawing slightly, he gave her shoulder a final pat. "I'll keep asking around," he couldn't stop himself from offering.

"Thank you, Grant."

He waited till she was steady on her feet, then opened the door to the restaurant for her. As she walked in, he thought of the woman who had caused all these problems.

Helen. For a moment he was sorry she'd perished in the avalanche. She ought to be here, facing these questions. But from what he'd seen and what he'd heard from Amalie, Helen had never been that good at coping with the consequences of her actions.

Davin was a prime example of that.

AMALIE OPTED NOT to join the snowshoeing excursion. She suspected Grant was a little disappointed with her decision, but Denise's resentment at seeing the two of them together had been obvious, and Amalie wanted time to think about the situation and where it was headed.

She and Grant *had* been spending a lot of time together recently. Many of their outings revolved around Davin. But many of their conversations and the glances they exchanged did not.

Was Grant interested in her? Amalie's rusty feminine instincts told her yes. What concerned her, however, were the feelings she'd been having for Grant. That morning at the avalanche shoot, her fear for his safety had gone beyond what was reasonable for someone she'd known such a short time.

Despite her relative inexperience in such matters, and her sense that they hadn't known each other long enough, Amalie suspected what was happening.

She was falling in love.

Maybe she shouldn't be surprised. Grant was a man in a thousand. Watching him try to deal with his torn loyalties for Ramsey and Denise and at the same time balance his concern for her feelings, Amalie had felt such affinity for him. So many times she'd found herself in the middle, too. Between her parents and Helena; between her parents and Davin.

What tugged at her heart the most was how much he cared, how hard he worked at doing the right thing. A man like that would be easily trapped by a woman who played on his sense of honor and compassion.

She couldn't do that. Grant deserved a truly exceptional woman. Not someone he felt sorry for, someone he felt he had to look out for and protect. Grant deserved an equal; a woman who shared his love of the mountains, with an adventurous spirit and the spunk to be his full partner.

Unfortunately, she was not that woman, and she only had to remember the fear she'd felt this morning to know she never could be.

Then there was her sister's reputation to consider. In the two months she'd lived here, Helena had done some terrible things, made some grievous mistakes. Amalie still liked to think those choices were not indicative of the person Helena had been. But clearly Grant did, and that hurt.

So did having the people of Revelstoke paint her with the same brush they'd used on Helena. Just because she and her sister looked like carbon copies, people thought they were the same inside. All their lives they'd run into that kind of thinking. Denise Carter was just one example.

The situation was a mess, Amalie acknowledged. A mess she could do very little about. She didn't see how she could stop caring about Grant, no matter how hard she tried. Even now, knowing she'd done the right thing, she was acutely disappointed at having passed on the afternoon outing with him.

Still, the free time was a bonus and she had to make the most of it. She phoned her lawyer, her parents and the boy she'd hired to shovel the walks and take in the mail back home.

Then she looked up the number for the local library to order the books Davin was interested in. While she had the phone directory out, impulse made her flip to the C section. Carter, Ramsey. His phone number and address were both listed, and she made note of them before slipping on her coat and going out to the car.

"You are not acting like a sane person," she told herself as she negotiated unfamiliar streets with the aid of a small map she'd picked up from the information center. After crossing the Illecillewaet River on Fourth Street, she drove as far as the hospital before turning left into an affluent, wooded neighborhood. She found the Carters' house on a crescent that backed onto forest and decided to park a few houses away.

The house was a story and a half with a double garage. The wood exterior was stained a dark reddish-brown, the trim an attractive deep green. The place looked tidy, well maintained, including the row of cedars that grew along the driveway.

Who had kept those cedars so perfectly shaped? Likely Ramsey, and she felt a pang for the other life, besides Helena's, that had been wasted so needlessly.

Amalie glanced at the digital clock in her car, realizing that it was almost this exact hour that she'd experienced the strange sensation of suffocating at Jeremy Mitchell's birthday party, just over two weeks ago.

Oh, Helena. Why did you have to die? You didn't even like skiing. I know you didn't. So what were you doing out there?

Tears fell, and Amalie let them. All her life she'd tried to protect Helena, and all her life she'd failed. Especially after Davin's birth. It was too easy to blame Helena for not keeping in touch; she herself should have made more effort.

Privately, she'd always thought it was better for all concerned if Helena stayed away. Now she won dered if she'd been motivated by more selfish reasons than she'd ever admitted to. Maybe she'd been scared of what would happen if Helena ever returned. Maybe she'd been afraid that once Helena saw Davin again she'd want him back.

Movement at the Carter house forced her thoughts to the present. The front door had opened. Now the little boy she'd seen that morning with Denise came outside, dressed in a hockey shirt and pants, a stick in one hand and a puck in the other. His boots left tracks in the thin film of snow that had fallen since the last time the walks were shoveled. He trudged to the center of the driveway, where a hockey net was positioned against the garage door.

For a long time he stood there, shoulders slumped, head bowed. Then he put the puck down and with his hockey stick slapped it into the net. In the living room window curtains moved as someone, probably Denise, kept watch over the little guy.

Immediately, Amalie knew this boy was not used to coming out alone to play hockey. In her mind she pictured his father standing in the net, calling out encouragement while Colin practiced his wrist shot.

For a moment, she felt a taste of Denise's rage. *Oh, Helena, how could you?*

GRANT DELIVERED an exhilarated Davin home shortly after seven. Amalie met them at the door dressed in a pale-gray sweatsuit, worry lines once again on her forehead, the only color in her face the blue of her eyes. Still, she summoned a smile for Davin and helped him pull off his outdoor clothing.

"Sorry we're late." He'd phoned earlier to warn her that Davin wasn't going to want to quit until it became too dark to snowshoe. Then they'd stopped for burgers at a drive-through.

"You should have come, Aunty. You wouldn't believe the size of those trees—what were they called, Grant?"

"Western red cedars."

Davin stretched his arms as far apart as they'd go. "Way bigger than this. We went on two different trails. Snowshoeing is even easier than skiing, but not as much fun."

"You've got a real athlete here." Grant patted the boy's back, then noticed the worry lines were not fading from Amalie's face. What had happened to get her so tense while they were gone? Or was she upset he'd kept Davin out too late?

"I'm glad you had fun, but now it's time to take a shower and head for bed."

"Go on if you want, Aunty." Davin grinned cheekily. "I'll stay up and talk to Grant."

She laughed. It was good to see. A little pink

tinged her cheeks, and those lines on her forehead were momentarily smoothed away.

"Good try." She swiveled Davin's shoulders till he was facing the short hall. "Now, march. There are clean towels waiting for you, and don't forget to brush and floss."

Her gaze followed him down the hall. When the door shut, her little spurt of positive energy fizzled. The frown was back, along with an uncharacteristic sag in her shoulders.

Grant decided to try apologizing again.

"I hope you weren't worried."

"No. I'm glad you called, though." She went to the sofa to fold an old afghan that he'd never noticed before. Somehow she ended up sitting, and he sat beside her.

"Are you okay?"

"Sure, Grant. I'm fine."

She didn't look at him, though, and he just couldn't believe her. He didn't know what to do. Probably he should leave and let her get some rest, but he didn't think fatigue was getting her down. She was upset, and maybe she needed to talk.

"So how did you spend your afternoon?"

"Oh, I made a few phone calls, ran a few errands...."

She was affecting a bright tone that he'd never heard before. Something *was* wrong. When she angled her shoulder slightly away from him, he guessed she didn't want him to see her face.

"Missing your sister?"

A small hiccup made him certain she was holding back tears. Instinctively, he put out his arm and drew her close. For a second she softened into him, and he was able to touch her hair, the side of her cheek, with his free hand.

"I'm sorry, Amalie."

She jerked out of his embrace and stood so quickly he wondered if he'd somehow hurt her. He watched as she fiddled with the blinds while the sound of water drumming against porcelain came from the bathroom. Moments later they heard exuberant, youthful vocalizations.

Amalie managed a smile. "He always sings in the shower. I don't think he has any idea how sound travels in this small apartment."

Grant listened for a moment, trying to make out the tune. "Maybe we should work on singing lessons, now that he's mastered snowshoes."

Amalie looked ready to laugh again, but the sound that came out was a sob. She turned her back to him, raised her hands to her face.

He was up and across the room in an instant. "Hey, I'm sorry. His voice isn't *that* bad."

"Oh, Grant..."

This time she let him hold her longer, even allowing her neck to bend in a little when he circled her shoulders with his arms.

"Why did Helena come here?" she asked. "Why did she have to die?"

Grant knew answers weren't expected. He was glad when she let herself cry a little, but not surprised when she pulled herself together after just a few short minutes.

"Oh, Lord, this is embarrassing. Now your shirt is damp."

He ran his index finger under her eyes, blotting her tears. "I'm not complaining."

She smiled, but kept her eyes lowered from his. "Grant...I've been thinking."

"Don't." He pulled her back close, his urge to comfort this woman shifting to something more elemental. "Amalie, look up at me. Let me kiss you."

"No." She lowered her head even farther, but she didn't push away.

"Don't you want to?"

"Of course I do. But Grant, we can't just kiss each other because we feel like it."

In her earnestness to convince him, she'd raised her head. It was all the opening he needed. Quickly he pressed his lips to hers, just one light touch, that he hoped was preliminary. Then he drew back and checked her expression.

"Why not?"

CHAPTER ELEVEN

AMALIE FELT RELUCTANT, but not resistant, in Grant's arms. He dared to pull her closer, to bend his head until his lips were an inch from hers.

She had no answer to his question. And when her eyes shut, he knew he had momentary sway over that stern voice at the back of her head. Perhaps it was her strict *parents'* voice, telling her it was wrong to do something just because it was *fun.*

Their lips met and joined, and he breathed her in, tasted her, like the fresh warm air that blew off the mountains in the spring. He bundled cool silky hair in one hand, then placed the other in the curve of her lower back.

That her hands were on him was a joy, too. One at his neck, one round his waist. Her thumb stroked the side of his jaw as she angled her face, deepening their kiss.

Then a thundering silence made them realize the water had just been shut off in the shower. She jerked back.

"I'm such an idiot—" She turned away, paced a few steps, then faced him again.

Color was all over her face now—a bright, hot pink. It was in her lips and across her cheeks, and even in the hollow at the base of her neck.

"When will it be safe to recover my sister's body? I really need to know."

"Oh, Amalie…" He was so disappointed he felt he himself could have shed a tear. Barriers. More barriers. Just when he thought they were getting closer, she'd pulled back, retrenching like the soldier she was.

"You know that's why we're here. What we're waiting for."

In other words, he wasn't to think their relationship was going anywhere. He began to see that he was the one who was acting the fool. When had she ever given him any real encouragement? "I don't know. There's been a lot of snow this week."

"It never stops, does it?" She sounded bitter now, standing at the window, playing with the blinds again, opening what she'd just recently closed. The room was so dark they could see the white crystals falling slowly through the yellow pool of a nearby streetlight.

"I can go check out the area tomorrow," he told her, making a promise he'd rather not have had to make. "I can't make any guarantee beyond that."

"I don't want to put any lives at risk. But I *do* want Helena's body found. Everywhere I turn in this town, I seem to come up with more questions than answers. Maybe Helena will have something on her, some papers or additional identification, that will help me figure out what she was doing here, where she came from, where she was going.''

The bathroom door slammed. They both turned to see Davin in his pajamas. He must have been more tired from the day than Grant had thought, because his face was white and his eyes were red.

''I'm going to bed now. Thanks for everything, Grant.''

Amalie stepped forward. ''Want me to tuck you in?''

''Nah, that's okay.'' He raised a hand in farewell, then shut himself into the second bedroom.

''I have to keep reminding myself he's growing up.'' It almost seemed Amalie was talking to herself. ''Next year he'll be in junior high....''

''Well, he's a good kid. I'm sure you won't have any trouble.''

''I hope not, Grant. It's just that...''

''Yes?''

''Well, now that Helena's dead, there's no way left to find out about his father. I wonder if he's thought about that at all.''

DAVIN STOOD BACK from his bedroom door, frowning at his aunt's final words. She probably hadn't realized he could hear her through the closed door.

Was there any way *they* had heard *him* singing in the shower?

He felt his face grow hot at the possibility. He'd been pretending he was one of the Backstreet Boys. Most guys his age didn't like their music—at least they didn't admit it at school. But he did.

Could they have heard? No—the sound of the water would have been too loud. Reassured, he flicked on the light from the small bedside lamp Amalie had set up next to his sleeping bag and reached for the book he'd borrowed from Grant's office. He tried to start reading where he'd left off, but the overheard conversation played back in his mind.

His father. For a moment Davin tried to imagine what the man might look like. But all he saw was a dark silhouette.

Sometimes he wondered what had been wrong with him that neither his real mother nor his father had wanted anything to do with him. He hadn't been an ugly baby. He'd seen the pictures, and they seemed pretty cute, as far as he could tell.

His aunt had told him his mother and father had been too young for the responsibility of raising a kid. Well, his aunt was exactly the same age as Helena. So why had she been able to take him, and not them?

Sometimes, when he was younger, Davin had daydreamed about his father coming back into his life. But he hadn't done it often, because he'd been scared that if his father did, he would take Davin away from Aunt Amalie.

"That couldn't happen, Davin," his aunt had re assured him when he'd finally confessed his fears. He'd been about seven at the time.

"I adopted you when you were born," she said. "Legally, I *am* your mother."

Then why can't I call you that? He asked his aunt all sorts of questions, but he was never brave enough to ask her that one. Maybe she was saving the name in case she got married and had real kids of her own.

"AMALIE, WOULD YOU do me a favor and tell me what's going on?"

Grant was pacing her sister's living room like a frustrated mountain lion. The image was disturbing, but thrilling, also. When she'd decided their relationship had to be curtailed, she hadn't stopped to think he might have an opinion on the subject, too.

"When I kiss you," he stopped to say, "it feels like you enjoy it. When you look at me, I get the impression you like me. Yet every time we get closer, you pull back. I want to know—are you just not that interested? Or are you afraid?"

She couldn't lie and say she wasn't interested. But it wasn't fear that held her back; it was the knowledge of her own responsibilities. "I have a job in Toronto, Grant. Parents who need me, a child to raise. I warned you I wasn't interested in a casual affair.''

And yet, with his taste still on her mouth and the feel of his hands imprinted on her body, a casual affair held its own temptations. Just once, shouldn't she have that experience?

But ''just once'' was how mistakes were made. Mistakes that could have ramifications on the people who depended on her, like Davin and her parents.

''And I told you from the start my feelings aren't casual.''

He couldn't possibly know how he confused her when he said things like that! Amalie escaped to the kitchen, where she began to scrub down the already clean countertops. She heard Grant's footsteps and, despite her anger, felt a thrill when she sensed him behind her.

''Let's give this thing between us a chance,'' Grant said. ''If it doesn't work out, fine. But maybe it will.''

With nail-biting anticipation, she sensed him drawing closer, felt his breath warm a spot on the back of her head. Just when she was sure he was about to kiss her there, she turned to face him, putting a hand to either side of his face to stop him.

''I'm sorry, Grant, but don't you see? There's too much against us.'' At that moment, though, it was hard to care. She'd never known a man like Grant. Strong, brave, unafraid of anything. The very fact that he was attracted to her made her will weaken almost as much as her legs.

"And what about the things going for us?" His eyes burned with possessive heat. "Like the way we feel about each other."

She saw the faulty link in his reasoning. "And how do you feel about me, Grant? You practically hated my sister. In some corner of your mind, aren't you afraid I'll turn out to be more like her than you first thought?"

For just a second his eyes shifted, and she knew the point was not moot.

"You are, aren't you? You worry that deep down, I'm just like Helena. That one day you might turn your head and find me dancing on the kitchen table, flaunting my body."

"What?"

She could see that he'd heard the stories, too. She'd been shocked when Toby Ward had described her sister's behavior They'd run into each other at the library—the last place she would have expected to meet the outgoing bartender. Which only reminded her of the danger of judging people too quickly.

Something everyone in this town had done to Helena.

"Come on, Grant. I know you've heard about my sister's...table dancing."

"And what does that have to do with you? Or with the way I feel?" His hands were on *her* face now, tilting it to meet his.

"I—" Amalie didn't know. Her thoughts were suddenly scattered.

"Maybe you should dance on a kitchen table sometime, Amalie. Maybe it's more fun than you think. Maybe you'd be darn good at it."

Somehow, somewhere, she'd taken the wrong tack. She wasn't scaring him off. She was *encouraging* him.

And this time when he kissed her, his need was all passion. Amalie caught her breath, then oxygen suddenly seemed irrelevant as he crushed his mouth to hers, lifting her body with his strong, capable arms.

There was no way she could fight against this, any more than a tender tree could arrest an advancing brush fire. Giving in was her only option. And oh, what a part of heaven surrender turned out to be.

Then the phone rang.

GRANT TURNED AWAY from Amalie as she reached for the receiver. Grasping the counter with both hands, he hung his head, trying to master the passion that had made him go after her like that.

He'd always viewed himself as a levelheaded guy. If Amalie said she wasn't interested, then it made sense to back off. Not to kiss her like a lust-crazed Neanderthal.

The really amazing thing, though, was that she'd kissed him with equal ardor. Talk about mixed messages.

"That's okay," he heard her say over the phone. "I was hoping—"

She'd told him she wasn't involved with anyone. Yet jealousy flared when she glanced at him, then away, twisting so her back was to him, her words a little more muffled.

He walked out of the room to give her privacy, curbing his curiosity by focusing on the promise he'd made earlier to check out the site where Helen and Ramsay had been killed.

Another damn promise. He thought of the one he'd made to Denise, renewed today in front of Blaine's Pizza Paradise. To find out how long Helen and Ramsey had been seeing each other.

God, he was such a fool to have agreed to that one. How could he possibly win? No matter how long Ramsey had been conducting his affair, Denise would still feel hurt. He should have told her to forget about it, to remember Ramsey for the good times in their marriage, not this last foolish aberration.

It would have been the right thing to say, but no,

he couldn't bring himself to be so blunt. And Grant knew why. Women in distress always flustered him. Except, he realized suddenly, for Amalie. When she'd been upset earlier, he hadn't felt uncomfortable at all. Just so sad for her.

Realizing he'd been pacing again, Grant stopped by the living room window. Although he wasn't trying to hear, Amalie's voice traveled clearly from the other room.

"No, really. It's not too late. I'm glad you called."

He heard her hang up the phone.

She came into the room with a weird expression, a combination of shock and disbelief.

"That was my lawyer in Toronto," she said. "They've traced my sister to an address in Seattle."

He went to her, cupped her shoulders. "Well, that's good. Isn't it?"

"I'm not sure." Amalie wavered slightly, and he tightened his grip. "There was someone else at that address. A man."

With one deep breath she pulled herself together, looked him square in the eyes.

"I guess your friend Ramsey wasn't the only one having an extramarital affair. My sister was married, too."

CHAPTER TWELVE

"HELEN WAS MARRIED," Grant repeated slowly.

Amalie waited as he mentally adjusted to the news. He would think even less of her sister now, and she couldn't really blame him. It was bad enough that Helena had been seeing a married man. That she was married herself made it so much worse.

Gently, Amalie slipped out from under Grant's hands. Now it was she who paced the living room floor, struggling to assimilate all the lawyer had said.

"I'm not sure I get it." Grant appeared confused. "If she had a husband, what was she doing here alone? Were they separated?"

"That part's not very clear." As if any part was. According to the lawyer, Helena had been married for three years. Three years! Surely at least once in that period she might have mentioned the guy. Let alone invited her family to the wedding.

Oh, Helena! The gulf between her and her sister had never felt so wide.

"Stand still for a minute." Grant reached out,

grasped hold of her arm. "You've got to calm down, Amalie."

If the phone hadn't rung, we'd be making love right now....

Amalie moved slightly, dislodging his hold on her. Maybe the timing of that phone call had been providential. After all, Davin was in the apartment. Sleeping in the room right next to them.

Oh, what was happening to her? Was she losing all her judgment, her good sense?

"What else did the lawyer say?" Grant asked.

Amalie focused her thoughts. "Well, her husband's name is Matthew Stanway." *Matthew.* That was a good, solid name. But what was he really like? There had to be a reason Helen had run away from him.

"What does Matthew do in Seattle?"

"I'm not sure. He works in the computer industry. It seems he just got back from a two-week business trip in Europe. My lawyer had left a message on his machine, and he called right away." She wrapped her arms around her chest and wondered about her sister's husband. Did he know Helena had a twin sister? Parents who lived in Ontario?

A son?

"So were they separated?"

She shrugged. "According to Matthew, he arrived home from work one day to find her and her car gone. A note stated she was leaving him, but she gave no explanation. They'd had no fights, no disagreements. He waited a week, figuring she'd probably return. But when she didn't, he hired a private investigator to find her.''

''Obviously, the investigator came up empty.''

''Seems he started off on the wrong track. Matthew was certain Helena would have gone to Vancouver. She was a Canadian citizen and they had friends there.''

From things the lawyer had said, Amalie had the impression that Matthew was quite wealthy. Which explained the jazzy sports car, the expensive jewelry. Thank God.

''I wonder if he's telling the whole story. It doesn't seem reasonable that she would just up and take off unless something was wrong.''

''I agree,'' Amalie said. ''And she was careful not to leave a trail—remember she didn't use credit cards.''

Amalie thought back over the past few months. That fissure of anxiety she'd felt in the weeks before Christmas must have been when her sister had left Stanway. But if Helena had been scared of him, if he'd been mean or abusive, wouldn't Amalie have picked up on those negative vibes before Helena ran off?

''Surely the police could have traced her to your parents and to you. I'm surprised you weren't notified that your sister was missing.''

"But the police were never involved. They told Stanway that since Helena had left of her own free will there was nothing they could do."

"If Matthew Stanway's story is true, he must have gone through hell."

"We'll have a chance to make our own assessment soon enough. Matthew intends to come to Revelstoke when Helena's body is found."

Grant shook his head, as if he couldn't believe it. "Great."

"Grant, I want to go with you when you check out the avalanche site tomorrow."

"That isn't a good idea. You know how much you hate being in the mountains. Why would you want to put yourself through that?"

It was a good question, one she had no clear answer for. "Just once I have to go there."

"That's nuts. You're not a strong skier, and the terrain is difficult and crosses several large avalanche paths."

Amalie felt her courage falter. Everything he said was true. It wasn't logical for a novice skier to purposefully go out in avalanche country.

But she wouldn't be alone. Grant would be there.

"It's something I have to do."

Grant's expression was contemplative. "I wonder, if the situation were reversed, would Helen feel the same sense of obligation toward you?"

"That doesn't matter."

"Doesn't it?"

"Oh, Grant. When it comes to Helena, you're so determined to see the worst in her."

"I see what's before me, that's all."

His hard line hurt, especially since she knew he had grounds for his opinions. That he was wrong was something she would have to prove. If possible.

"I have to go, Grant."

"You'll only slow me down. On my own I could get up and back in one day. With you along we'll have to stay overnight at the hut where Ramsey and Helena…"

"Please take me, Grant. I know you're right—I'll slow you down. But if I could see the place where she died, just once…I think it would help me believe she's really gone."

Grant stared at her a long minute, gauging the measure of her determination. "I must be crazy to even consider—"

"Yes!" She grabbed his arm.

"You'll need equipment. We'll have to postpone the trip a day while we outfit you."

She didn't like the idea of a delay. "Couldn't I just make do with my rentals?"

"No way. Amalie, this isn't the Summit Trail we'll be on. You need proper gear and I have to give you a little basic ski and safety instruction.

After all, you've never used skins, although you have downhill-skied and that will help.''

Skins? Since she didn't know what he was talking about, she decided not to argue further. "When will we be able to leave?"

"The day after tomorrow. Early."

Amalie decided she'd better be happy with that.

OVERNIGHT THE WIND SHIFTED, bringing colder, drier air to the interior of the Selkirks. Grant could smell the change in the humidity when he awoke before dawn, on Tuesday morning.

"Bloody cold," he grumbled, abandoning his covers to shut the window he liked to keep open when he slept. The furnace, on a timer to kick in at 4:30 a.m., was already blasting hot air from the register. He placed his feet on the metal grating and let the heat travel up his legs.

Amalie. These days most of his conscious thoughts revolved around her. Today, he had the happy prospect of spending hours with her, outfitting her for the trip and taking her on a trial run.

The joy he felt, however, was a worry itself.

"You're being a fool, Thorlow. Setting yourself up for another fall." Amalie had made it plain their relationship wasn't going anywhere. Revelstoke was about the last place she'd want to settle, and he wasn't prepared to move for any woman. Twice before he'd been tested on this, and each time had remained firm.

Sometimes he thought about those women. Tory, who'd wanted him to relocate to Vancouver while she articled and studied for the bar. And Sandra, who'd worked for over a year on avalanche control, then had wanted him to explore the world with her. But he'd already done that—with his parents, then later as a young man before he'd settled into his present job.

After each of the botched relationships he'd promised himself not to get involved with another woman unless she was as committed to these mountains, this place, as he was.

So it didn't make sense to fall head over heels for a cool blonde with a life anchored in Toronto— just about the last place he'd ever consider moving to in Canada. Especially when the blonde had a twin sister who'd caused more trouble in two months than most people created in a lifetime.

Grant shuffled to the bathroom and faced his reflection. "You're an idiot. Do you realize that?" He squeezed out a measure of toothpaste, which promptly fell off his toothbrush into the sink. Grant scooped it back onto the bristles and rinsed it under cold water.

Last night Amalie couldn't have been more clear. The relationship was going nowhere; she didn't want to make love with him.

Knowing that, he'd agreed to take her with him, to spend the night together at the Asulkan Hut.

Spending the night with her, *in separate sleeping bags,* was going to be torture.

Grant rinsed out his mouth, his toothbrush, then turned on the shower. Maybe they wouldn't spend the night apart. Amalie *was* attracted to him; she hadn't tried to deny it. With the two of them alone on the mountain, surely it was at least *possible* something might happen.

Mentally, he added a couple of items to his packing list. Grant was the kind of guy who liked to be prepared. For any and all contingencies.

Remote though they might be.

He wondered if she had any idea of the rustic conditions they would be facing. He'd tried to warn her last night, but obviously been unable to dissuade her.

Stubborn lady.

But that was one of the qualities he admired about her. Forcing yourself to do something that terrified you took real courage. Even coming here, all the way from Toronto, had taken guts. Yet Amalie never gave herself the credit she deserved.

With a sigh of resignation he hauled himself out of the shower and picked up his razor. As he ran the blade over his cheeks, down the side of his neck, he noticed his hair was getting a little shaggy.

He yanked at the top drawer under the cabinet, pulled out the scissors, then paused.

He wondered if Amalie was the kind of woman to notice such details. In case she was, it wouldn't hurt to get a proper haircut this time.

He put the scissors back in the drawer and headed to the kitchen. The coffee, also on an automatic timer, was ready. Grant poured a cup, wishing he could get his toaster automated, as well, so that two crisp slices—already buttered and slathered with jam—slid onto a plate the minute he walked in the room.

One of his favorite movies was that old one from Disney where the absentminded professor had his whole kitchen hooked up with gizmos and gadgets that took care of all the mundane little jobs that Grant, too, found so tiresome.

Today he settled on grabbing a box of cereal from the cupboard and eating it by the handful as he went to the spare room, where his computer— with its link to the office information systems—was just waiting for the touch of his fingers to come alive.

Weather forecasts had been revised overnight. Now the projection was for cold, clear weather in the foreseeable future. Unbelievably, it seemed they had a window of opportunity when conditions would be ideal for backcountry traveling.

Grant shut down the computer and took another

handful of dry cereal, chasing it with a gulp of strong, hot coffee.

Thank God the weather, at least, was cooperating. He didn't need extra complications on this trip. Taking along a novice would be challenge enough, beginning with assembling the gear she would need.

Sometime during the day he also had to fit in a couple of hours at the office and a trip to the hospital where Ramsey had worked. Maybe someone there would know when his affair with Helen had begun.

"I GUESS THIS IS IT," Amalie said to Davin and Heidi, who were waiting in the apartment building vestibule with her Wednesday morning. She clamped down on her nerves as she watched Grant's truck stop just outside her apartment building. She was unsure about her ability to make it up the mountain and anxious about seeing the place where Helena had died. Most of all she was concerned about spending the night alone with Grant.

She picked up the small bag of essentials that Grant had told her she was allowed to bring. He already had her skis, which he'd stowed after their practice workout yesterday afternoon.

Mountaineering skis, she'd discovered, were a hybrid between cross-country and downhill. Skins—a velvety fabric that was glued onto the bottoms—provided traction for climbing. There was also a mechanism that allowed the heel to stay attached to the ski, providing more stability for descending steep slopes.

"I'll miss you," she said, giving Davin a quick hug. Heidi had planned an afternoon skiing outing on Summit Road, followed by an evening of horror movies, but Davin was still disgruntled about missing the backcountry trip.

Grant was already loping up the sidewalk. A second later, he'd pulled open the front door and entered amid a burst of frosty air.

"Ready and waiting, I see." His gaze swept them all, stopping sympathetically at Davin.

"Next trip, you'll definitely come along," he promised.

Davin nodded, his disappointment so acute he was unable to bring his gaze up from the floor.

Amalie squeezed his slender shoulders. "Would you carry this to the truck for me, Davin? I just want to remind Heidi of a few things."

He nodded, taking the small pack from her hands. Once he was out the door, Amalie turned to Grant.

"You said there was a number where Heidi could reach us in case of an emergency?"

"I have it written out here." He pulled off his glove, then retrieved a slip of paper from his pocket. "One more thing, Heidi?" He cleared his throat.

Alerted by the nervousnous of his voice, Amalie paused on her way out the door.

"Did, uh, Ramsey ever come to this apartment to visit Helen?"

Amalie went still. So Grant was still on his fact-finding mission for Denise Carter. She supposed she ought to be grateful he wasn't doing his snooping behind her back anymore. She wondered if he'd told Denise yet that Helena had been married.

"Why do you ask?" Heidi's tone matched the sharp look in her eyes.

Grant raised his eyes to the ceiling as he sighed. "Denise wants to know how long they were seeing each other."

"Denise Carter wants to know, does she?" Heidi fingered the zipper of her outermost sweater. She was dressed in layers, all ready for her afternoon on the trails. "Well, she could have asked me out-right. But I suppose she's still pretty shook up. You tell her I never saw them together. Certainly Ramsey wasn't one of the young studs who used to gather at those parties Helen threw."

"Thanks, Heidi. Appreciate the information."

Heidi nodded, then clapped him on the back. "Sometimes a man can be too much of a gentle-man, Grant. You remember that."

Outside, Amalie said a final farewell to Davin,

then climbed into the truck, settling into the seat while Grant closed the door after her. They drove away with Heidi and Davin both waving, one more enthusiastically than the other.

Amalie snapped on her seat belt, then looked sideways at Grant. He'd slipped on sunglasses against the low morning sun. Aware of her perusal, he smiled at her. "Feel bad about leaving Davin?"

"Yes. He's gone on sleepovers at his friend's house before, but this is the first time *I've* left *him*."

"First time in eleven years?"

"Well, yes. Is that so strange?"

Grant just shrugged, and Amalie turned her gaze to the highway. The roads were clear; the sun was shining. It seemed like a favorable omen for their trip. Reminded of something else, she turned back to Grant.

"What do you suppose Heidi meant with that last comment of hers about being too gentlemanly?" she asked.

"I'm not sure," he said. "I suppose she could have meant that I was being a fool to gather information on Ramsey and Helen for Denise."

Yes. That was what she'd thought, too.

"Or..." He raised his sunglasses to shoot her a piercing look. "She could have been talking about you and me spending the night alone together on the mountain."

Oh, my Lord! "I guess she has no way of knowing we packed separate sleeping bags."

Once more Grant took her attention from the road to glance at her. "Those bags can be zipped together, Amalie."

"Really?" Amalie turned the heater control on the front panel down a notch. "How inventive."

CHAPTER THIRTEEN

AMALIE DID HER BEST to avoid staring at the stern profile of the surrounding mountain peaks as Grant parked his truck at the base of the Asulkan Trail. He turned off the ignition, then shifted in his seat.

"Last chance to back out."

"As if." She opened her door and stepped out onto hard-packed snow. *You asked for this,* she reminded herself, hitching her pack—significantly lighter than Grant's—onto her back.

"Let's check the beepers," Grant said, flipping on the power to the avalanche beacons they would be wearing throughout their trip.

Yesterday, during her crash course on avalanche safety, Grant had explained how the transceivers sent out a signal that rescuers could use to locate skiers who'd been completely buried during an avalanche.

"Were Helena and Ramsey wearing these?" she asked. The transceiver felt heavy in her hand, although it was only the size of a large cell phone.

"Probably, but we can't be sure. We weren't able to get close enough to the site to test for a signal.

And we may not be able to this time, either. Of course, the batteries might be dead by now. Depends how fresh they were when they started out.''

In one fluid motion, Grant shouldered his own pack. She'd checked out the items earlier and knew he carried, besides their sleeping bags and food, a first-aid kit, large snow shovel, sectional aluminum probes, a snow saw and an avalanche cord.

''Okay?'' He raised his sunglasses to scrutinize her expression.

''You bet.'' Amalie made herself speak with a confidence she wasn't feeling. She felt dwarfed by the snow-capped trees around her, let alone the towering mountains that dominated the landscape in every direction.

''Good.'' He smiled, then brushed a gloved hand against her cheek. ''Just to give you a quick orientation, that's the Sir Donald Range to the east, the Asulkans to the west. We'll be heading mostly south, alongside Asulkan Brook, toward Youngs Peak. The trail starts nice and easy but gets pretty steep about four kilometers in.''

Amalie wondered what he meant by *pretty steep*. Once more she suffered doubts.

''It's not too late to change your mind.''

''Would you stop saying that? I can do this, Grant.'' *Yeah, right.*

He smiled with grudging respect. ''Of course you can. Okay, then. Let's go.''

Amalie started moving, following in Grant's tracks. Cold wind skimmed over her skin, ruffling the loose strands of hair that had already escaped the long braid hanging down her back. Bright sunlight, its power magnified by the stark white snow, made it impossible for her to open her eyes without the protective sunglasses they'd bought yesterday.

Her trip with Grant to a mountain-equipment store had precipitated another round of expenditures she couldn't really afford. But at the moment, money was the least of her worries.

If anything happened to her, there would be no one left for Davin. That was the worry that nagged at the back of her mind, that had made forcing down breakfast this morning such a chore.

Poor Davin, she was really all he had. And if her parents did agree to take him in out of some sense of duty, she knew they would never love him the way she did.

Even her desperate need to understand what had happened to Helena, though, wouldn't have been enough to convince her to come on this trip if not for Grant.

She focused on the man who was breaking trail in front of her, the man she was now trusting with her life, and, in a sense, Davin's life too.

Despite her fear, she knew he would keep them both safe.

IF HELENA DID THIS, then so can I, Amalie told herself, as she pushed one foot in front of the other, trying to ignore the burning in her quadriceps.

With the change in terrain, they'd stopped about an hour ago to attach skins to the bottom of their skis, and Amalie gave silent thanks for the wonderful fabric that allowed the skis to slide smoothly in one direction and provided resistance against backsliding.

"Look, you can see the glacier ahead." Grant had stopped to point out the impressive field of white ice.

Amalie put her arm to her forehead and nodded. Pushing through her chest-tightening fear came a small thrill of excitement. The glacier sat astride some impressive peaks, and now Grant identified them like old friends.

"That's the Rampart, the Dome, Mount Jupiter."

Magnificent names for magnificent structures. Amalie's breath caught and held as her gaze swept over them. Then, from nowhere, came the choking fear that had overtaken her at Jeremy's party. The mountains and trees combined to form prison walls from which there was no escape.

She was trapped. They were trapped. And there was so little air. Of course it would be thinner at this altitude. She tried to breathe faster to compensate.

"Are you okay?"

"Yes." She gasped. "Yes. I think…maybe a little claustrophobic."

Grant put his arm around her shoulders. "Take a deep breath. Release slowly."

"I'm so-sorry." She filled her lungs with air, then let it out in a slow stream. "I'm holding you up again." Despite her efforts to push herself to the limit, she'd had to stop a lot. Over and over Grant had had to wait for her to catch up. They'd taken several breaks when she'd known he could have easily pushed on.

"Hey, it's okay. I budgeted time for this." He eased her back to the natural ledge provided by a fallen tree. "Sit. We'll have a snack and a little water."

Amalie sank down with a sigh. "My legs thank you, my lungs thank you, my stomach thanks you." She took the water bottle Grant offered and drank eagerly. Before her was a postcard view of jagged mountain peaks blanketed with pristine white snow, contrasting with a sky of piercing, translucent blue.

Beautiful, yes, but terrifying, too. She shifted her attention to her companion and thought that, all things considered, he was much safer to concentrate on.

He appeared relaxed as he shuffled through the pack for trail mix. His color was normal, as was his breathing. She wondered what it was like to be in such good condition, and how she could fit regular exercise into her already frenetic schedule at home.

Home. How far away it seemed now—their little duplex in Bloor West Village, with its inviting front porch and pretty wooden shutters. Again she mused that the money she'd spent these past few weeks had pushed her goal of ownership even further into the future. The knowledge should have depressed her. But at the moment, she was too exhausted to care.

"Are we halfway?"

"Almost." Grant glanced toward the west. "Don't worry. We'll make it before dark."

The idea of being in these mountains during the night terrified her. But she'd worry about that later, find comfort in the fact that Grant didn't seem at all concerned. He tilted his head back to take a drink, then brushed the moisture from his mouth with his hand.

For a moment their glances caught, and in the bright sun she glimpsed traces of green in his eyes that she'd never noticed before.

"We'll be traveling across huge avalanche paths," he said. "I think I've picked a safe route, but just to be careful, we should start skiing a little farther apart."

Yesterday he'd explained that this was standard procedure in avalanche territory. In case one of them triggered a release of the snow pack, the other wouldn't be caught up in the same slide. She'd thought it a reasonable precaution then. But out here in the wilds she was scared to death.

"How do you do it?"

"What?" Grant was fitting his water bottle back into a loop at the side of his pack.

"You have to be out in conditions like this all the time. Doesn't it ever frighten you?"

"I love this country," he said simply. "Have since I first saw it." He looked out to the peaks ahead of them and sucked in a deep breath of fresh air. "I feel so alive out here. Don't you feel it, too?"

What Amalie felt was the beginning of a bad headache, but she didn't dare tell Grant that. She didn't want to be the cause of any more delay. Darkness in this desolate wilderness was going to be bad enough. If they didn't make the hut, however, it would be a nightmare.

"SEE. I TOLD YOU WE'D MAKE IT."

Amalie raised her head but couldn't see what Grant was talking about. Her calves burned, her feet hurt and each forward step was agony. A throbbing pain had started at her temples, and her head felt so heavy she was surprised she didn't topple over with the weight of it.

Fatigue. She hadn't known the meaning of the

word until now, but as of today, she was intimately acquainted with it.

Push and glide. Push and glide. She moved ahead a few feet, then a few more. Now Grant was near enough that she could reach out an arm and touch his elbow.

"Are we close to the hut?"

"We're there." He sounded calm and confident, but Amalie wasn't fooled. She knew he'd been worried for a while.

"I still don't see it."

Grant pointed. She squinted. A patch of brown stood out against the white backdrop. Mobilizing her last resources, she moved forward again.

No wonder it had been hard to spot. The gentle A-line roof—fringed with thick, blue-tinged icicles—was weighed down by about four feet of dense white powder. Amalie and Grant left their skis outside, propped against the wall by the door.

The inside was basic. A table. Some chairs. Bunks to sleep about a dozen, and a propane stove for warmth. Amalie couldn't have cared less about the amenities. She'd made it.

Thump. Her backpack slid off her shoulders to the floor, and she followed. To think she'd worried about spending the night with Grant.

"Wake me when it's morning."

He laughed, stepping over her as if she were a puddle, to get to the stockpile of propane. "Oh, I think you'll revive before then. Just wait till I have this baby burning. You'll be surprised how much heat it puts out.''

''Whatever.'' Amalie shut her eyes, feeling the blessed relief of being able to relax all her muscles at the same time. She truly didn't know where Grant got his energy. After seven hours on the trail, he was hustling around the small hut, even humming as he unpacked cooking utensils from his apparently bottomless backpack.

Amalie concentrated on the tune, knowing she'd heard it recently. The lyrics still tantalizingly out of reach, she drifted off to sleep. It felt like seconds later that she opened her eyes, but she knew it had been longer. Grant had several pots boiling on top of the stove. They smelled *good*.

She sat up.

''Hey, you're looking better.'' Grant ripped open a small packet and added it to the largest pot. The aroma of chicken broth filled the hut.

''Lord, I don't think I've ever been so tired.''

''It's the fresh mountain air. And the altitude.''

''Like heck.'' She stretched out her arms, despite the objection from her muscles. ''It was the skiing. I guess I'm more out of shape than I thought.''

''It wouldn't take long to change that.''

She left his quiet statement unchallenged and perused the room. Any remnants of Helena and Ramsey's stay had long been cleared out. Amalie closed her eyes and tried to connect with the part of her that had always sensed when Helena was in trouble.

Nothing. That surprised her. Somehow she'd thought that once she got here... Well, maybe tomorrow, out on the mountain...

"Why do you figure Helena and Ramsey picked this spot for their tryst?" she asked. "A motel room would have been more comfortable."

"No motel could have matched this place for privacy and isolation." Grant covered the pot he'd been stirring, then faced her.

Making her all too aware that what had applied to one sister also applied to the other. She and Grant were completely alone in this place. Whatever happened, she wouldn't have to worry about Davin, or the landlady, or anybody else finding out.

Whatever happened...

Suddenly aware of the dark, she looked out the window and realized the sun had set for the evening. The old sensation of panic resurfaced. She gasped for air, but it was as if the oxygen had turned solid and could not enter her mouth. She thought about all that snow on the roof of the cabin. What if the wood gave under the pressure? They would be buried, suffocated, just like Helena and Ramsey.

"What's wrong?"

She pushed past Grant, lurching for the door. The cool sweep of a breeze was reassuring, but she was startled at how fast the outside world had disappeared under the cloak of darkness.

Night fell quickly in the mountains, Grant had warned, especially in the winter. Now she leaned with her back on the door frame and tried to suck in a full breath of air.

"Claustrophobia again?" Grant asked, coming up from behind and pressing a hand against her shoulder.

She nodded. "I can't go back in there."

"It's okay, Amalie. We can leave the door open for a while if it helps."

It wouldn't really. The world around them had been obliterated by the lack of sunlight. Amalie wrapped her arms around her middle.

"I can't see them anymore, but I can feel them."

"What?"

"The mountains." She shivered, knowing she was being fanciful. And it was ridiculous, because she prided herself on her practicality, yet here she was imagining the mountains glaring down at her in disapproval.

"It's because we don't belong here," she said. "They want us to leave."

"Amalie." Grant gave her a small shake. "You can't let it get to you. The night is going to be too long for you to spend it cringing in terror. Let me pour you some tea and then we can enjoy our 'gourmet' dinner."

She laughed at that. "Okay."

Another gulp of air, then she forced herself back into the cabin.

It was a little more inviting now. A red glow emanated from the center of the room, where the stove sat, and its welcoming warmth encouraged her to step closer. Grant had pulled two tin cups from his pack, and she wondered if she shouldn't be helping. But it was such a luxury to sit and relax.

"Thank you for bringing me along, Grant. I know I've been a pain…hardly pulling my own weight."

"You've been fine." His voice sounded a little gruff. "Better than I expected, actually." He passed her a full cup. "Hold it by the handle so you don't burn yourself."

She sat back on the sleeping bag, resting the cup on her bent knees.

"Black bean soup. Gouda cheese in pitas. And—" he held up a small, corked bottle "—a little red wine to go with it."

"Wine?" Amalie smiled. The evening had definitely just taken a turn for the better.

"THE SUMMER I WAS IN GRADE SEVEN," Grant said as he topped up Amalie's mug, "my parents and I went white-water rafting on the Colorado River. It was early spring, and the water was high and wild. I, of course, was determined to prove how brave I was. As our raft entered a narrow, rocky corridor, I stood up, along with the guides, to help steer.''

Amalie closed her eyes. She could picture him at that age, just one year older than Davin. He would be tall, all bones and sun-browned skin.

"I had no idea what I was doing, of course. I just wanted to impress a young girl I'd met on the trip. As I held my paddle out over the water, the raft shifted suddenly to one side. I fell out the other.''

Amalie untwined her arm from his in order to sip her wine. They were huddled together for warmth, although there was plenty of that now. She twisted her head to look up at him.

"Were you hurt?''

"No. Luckily, my head missed the rocks—but I lost my pants to the current. Boy, was I embarrassed when they hauled me back on board in my underwear.''

"I'll bet that girl was impressed, all right.''

Grant nuzzled her head with his chin. ''She let me kiss her when we were sitting around the bonfire later that night.'' He paused for a moment. ''Donna Lee was her name.''

"I think I'm jealous.'' Amalie said the words lightly, but in truth she was. A little. Not about the kiss, but for the adventures Grant had had when he was young.

"What did you do the next summer?''

"I think that's the one when we drove down to Mexico. Now, *that* was an experience."

"Is there any place you haven't been? Any place you haven't seen?"

"Sure. But I'm not that eager to travel anymore. I've had enough. That's what I like so much about this part of the world. I figure there's enough wilderness here to last me my whole life."

"What about your parents? Where are they now?"

"Touring South America. They retired to Puerto Rico."

"To a condo beside a nice golf course?" she teased.

"Actually, yes," he surprised her by saying. "But they're always leaving for just one more adventure."

Amalie wondered if her parents knew the meaning of that word. Or if she herself did, for that matter. When was the last time she'd experienced anything that could even remotely be called that?

Now, she realized. *This.* She felt a tingle of excitement as Grant began playing with her hair. He was uncording her braid, and as he did so, tension eased in pleasurable little tickles along her scalp.

"You have the hair of an angel," he said, before bending to place a kiss on the top of her head. She could feel his fingers, winding through the long strands and closed her eyes in bliss.

"This wine was a very good idea."

He placed a hand on her cheek, then brushed his lips against the base of her neck. "Who was your first love, Amalie?"

"I'm not sure I had one." She twisted in his arms, careful not to upset her mug of wine. "Protective parents, remember?"

He traced a finger down the short line of her nose, then gently outlined the shape of her lips. "But you don't live at home anymore."

No, she didn't. Still, recalling the handful of men she'd dated over the years, she didn't think any of them qualified as what she considered a "first love."

Amalie sighed as Grant stopped touching her and took a sip of his wine.

"What about you, Grant? Why haven't you married?"

"I'm not that old, only thirty-one." He cleared his throat. "The truth is, I'm not that good with women. I've tried to blame the fact that I insist on living in this remote part of the world, but it's really more than that."

"Not good with women?" Hadn't he noticed the way Denise Carter looked at him? Or how even crotchety old Mrs. Eitelbach glowed when he was in the room?

He swallowed back a little more wine. "I had this girlfriend in university. After graduation she stayed in Vancouver, while I moved out here. We tried to keep up the relationship long-distance.''

''And what happened?''

''When she passed her bar exam, she invited me to Vancouver to celebrate. I went, but it was a big mistake. The law firm where she worked put on this big party, and I must have stood out like a cowbird in a nest of robins. My clothes were wrong, my manners were wrong, everything I said was wrong. My girlfriend was embarrassed by me. We never saw each other again.''

''Oh, Grant.'' She could so easily see Davin in a similar circumstance and her heart bled for the young man Grant had been.

He told her another story then, about taking five months to cycle around Australia after he finished high school. As he talked, he played gently with her hair, occasionally brushing the side of her cheek or the tip of her nose.

Amalie's nerves were absolutely on edge. Each time his fingers touched her, no matter where or how innocently, a burning need blocked all other sensation from her mind.

Would they make love tonight? She'd come here thinking it was a situation to be avoided. Now, warmed by the fire and the hours they'd spent talking, she realized she'd never felt so in tune with another person. Making love with Grant seemed the most natural, inevitable outcome. Yes, she was nervous, but with Grant it would be okay. She just knew it.

The question was, did he still want her? His touches said yes, but he wasn't in any great hurry.

Finally, when the wine was done and he'd told her enough stories to fill a three-hundred-page travel book, she put her hand behind his head.

"Are you planning to talk *all* night?"

OUTSIDE, THE WIND HOWLED, but snow and mountains were the last subjects on Amalie's mind at the moment. Grant had undressed her in the rosy glow of the fire, and now he was zipping their sleeping bags together.

"Come here." He took her hand, his eyes on her body as he laid her on the bed he'd prepared.

The flannel was soft on her skin, and she put her fingers to her lips, which still burned from his kisses, then watched as he pulled his turtleneck over his head. The sculpted muscles of his chest gleamed in the glow from the stove, and she reached out to trace them with her hands.

Next off were his pants. He had no modesty as he tossed them to the side, no concern that he was now completely available for her to see.

Somehow, Amalie wasn't surprised. Grant was too comfortable with himself, so completely at home with his masculinity, that she couldn't picture him worrying about his body

It was hard to imagine what he could have worried about, had he been so inclined. He looked perfect to her, and the fact that he was so totally aroused made her own desire pulse that much stronger.

No, the odd thing was that *she* didn't feel self-conscious. Completely naked, utterly exposed to a man for the first time in her life. What was wrong with her? She didn't feel in the least shy or inhibited.

As if to prove it, she reached out and stroked a hand down the length of his chest, paused at the thickening of hair at his groin...then continued along the length of him. Here his skin was velvet soft, at odds with the ramrod alertness that caused his erection to stand out from his body.

He groaned softly at her touch, then caught her hand in his. "Amalie, you look like a Norse goddess." With an unhurrying touch, he stroked the mounds of her breasts, glided over the dip of her waist, then the swell of her hips.

He eased down on the sleeping bags, then proceeded to touch her everywhere—places that no one, until now, had ever known before. His touch was light, but oh so effective. Soon he brought her to a delicious paradox where the pleasure was so intense she didn't know how much more she could stand.

"Ready?" He whispered the request before rising above her. For a moment she wondered if she should warn him.

And decided, no.

CHAPTER FOURTEEN

HIS BODY STILL TWINED with Amalie's, Grant let his head fall back on the sleeping bag and wondered what the hell to say.

Why didn't you tell me? No—that would sound accusatory, make her think he was resentful or even angry. And hadn't she hinted? Telling him she didn't think she'd had a first love.

How was it possible? That would make her feel she'd done something wrong. But dammit, how *was* it possible? Sure her parents had been strict, but she was a beautiful woman and she'd been on her own for—how old was Davin?—at least eleven years.

"You think I'm weird, right?"

Amalie's head was tucked just under his chin, where he couldn't see her. He could feel the tension in her body and knew it was his fault for not having spoken the appropriately reassuring words, at the appropriate time.

"No." He squeezed her tightly. "I think you're beautiful, sexy and brave."

He knew he hadn't blown it when he felt her

muscles loosen. Her breath teased the hairs on his chest as she laughed softly.

"I'll give you beautiful and sexy." She propped her head up on her elbow to look down at him. "But not brave." The corners of her smile trembled, then gave way. "I've been scared every moment since we left your truck."

"I know." He pulled Amalie back inside the cocoon of warmth, gathering in the top of the bag to keep out the cold air. "I could see the fear in your face. But that only makes what you've done even more courageous. Not many people would force themselves to do something that scared them to death."

"I keep obsessing about all that snow on the roof," she said. "You're going to think I'm paranoid, but is there any chance it could cause the roof to cave?"

"These structures are built to withstand loads much greater than this. I could go out, though, and shovel it off if that would make you rest easier."

He felt her hand on the side of his face. "I don't want you to leave."

"And I don't want you to leave, either." He was talking about the future now, about her eventual return to Toronto. Given what had just happened between them, surely she might consider staying a while longer. Maybe renting the apartment long-term, applying for a job…

Ignoring the way her legs had stiffened beside him, he played what he saw as his trump card. "Davin seems happy here. And Revelstoke's a good place to raise kids."

"It's impossible, Grant."

She spoke as if he'd asked whether she could settle on the moon. And maybe he had. She didn't connect with the mountains the way he did. And coming from Toronto, well, Revelstoke probably seemed like a real hick town. Still—

"'Impossible' is a little strong, isn't it?"

"I've got my job and my parents to look after."

"We have a hospital in Revelstoke," he pointed out. "And your parents aren't that old, are they?"

"Early sixties. But they really depend on me, Grant. I'd feel terrible abandoning them."

"What about you and *your* happiness?"

She regarded him. "You could always move to Ontario."

He waited for her to laugh. "You're joking, right?"

"I'll admit I didn't expect you to jump at the offer."

"Amalie, if I moved, I wouldn't fit in. I don't know if I would even be *myself* in a big city like that."

"I know. It's okay, Grant. I understand." She spoke like a mother comforting a hurt child. But she snuggled up against his chest as though seeking that same reassurance for herself.

He was happy to oblige. Holding her to him, he tried not to worry about the next time he'd have the opportunity to make love to her. The thing was, to enjoy this moment.

But that wasn't easy. In his personal life, he didn't live for the moment. He was a thinker, a planner. And he had no doubt Amalie was the same. Her body remained tense next to his, and he wondered whether it was the uncertainty of their future or her fear of these mountains that had her so stressed.

He was struggling with a fear of his own now. Tomorrow they'd find out whether it was safe to mount a search party for her sister's body. If it was, he could have his team back up here by the end of the week. Once they found what they were looking for, Amalie and Davin would have no reason to prolong their stay.

Something he'd known from the start, of course. But that was before he'd started falling in love with her.

"THIS IS THE SPOT," Grant said the next morning. "We followed their tracks along this ridge, and here's where they disappeared down into that bowl."

He'd pointed out the landmarks earlier. Youngs

Peak, the Pterodactyl. Amalie's gaze followed the direction of his finger.

A wide swath ran down the mountain—the slidepath marked with chunks of snow and, lower down, uprooted pines that had been smashed into kindling, their needles scattered.

It was horrible. Just horrible. Leaning on her ski poles, Amalie thought of her sister, and relived what she'd felt that Sunday afternoon. The pain, the burning in her lungs, the panic…

For the first time since the avalanche, her sister's death seemed real to her.

Helena gone.

When they were six, Helena had been the first to lose a tooth. She'd been so proud and excited. Together they'd wrapped the small treasure in a lacy doily, then carried it in to show their mother.

It was, perhaps, the first time Helena had done something before her sister. Amalie had walked first, talked first, learned to read first. But Helena had this tooth. And even through her envy, Amalie had been glad for her.

Not their mother. "Did you get blood on that doily? For heaven's sake, Helena. You have no sense." That was the way things had been in their house. Nothing Helena did was ever right.

Amalie heard Grant ski up beside her, then felt his arm heavy over her shoulders. "Are you okay?"

She couldn't tear her eyes from the avalanche path. "Do you know when it happened?"

"Sometime Sunday afternoon. Of course we can't be sure of the exact hour."

"Twenty minutes after four, eastern standard time."

"What? I don't see how…"

"I was about to bust the badge off a papier-mâché sheriff." She remembered swinging the bat. Remembered how she'd stumbled when, expecting resistance, she'd met none.

"A sheriff? Amalie, I think it's the altitude. It can make even seasoned skiers a little light-headed."

"I'm fine, Grant. You don't believe I'm right about the time, do you?"

"Well, how could you know?" he asked, sounding reasonable.

"Helena and I had this way of communicating with each other. I don't know what to call it. Whenever I get the feeling—whenever I *got* the feeling—I just *knew* Helena was in trouble. "

"ESP?"

"I guess. The day of the avalanche, I was swinging at a piñata at a birthday party for a friend of Davin's, when suddenly I felt as if the air had been knocked out of me. I fell on the ground, and it took at least a minute for me to recover my breath. The whole time I felt something heavy was pressing down on me. But nothing was, Grant. I was just experiencing a milder version of what Helena was going through.''

She expected Grant to scoff, but he just stared. "This has happened before?"

"Yes." She recalled an earlier example. "Once when we were in elementary school Helena broke her arm during physical education. I wasn't at school that day—I was home with the flu—but I felt a terrible pain in my arm at the same time as her accident. There were other occurrences, too. When she went into labor..."

Amalie's hands went to her stomach, remembering the agony of those early contractions.

"Helena had a terrible time giving birth to Davin. The complications were serious and very rare. She almost died on the delivery table, then later when she began to hemorrhage.''

"Did you experience that pain, too?"

"Not once I was with her. The hospital called and I came as soon as I could. These transmissions between us usually only happened when we were apart.''

Amalie felt cold at the corner of her eyes where tears were gathering. That kind of communication was in the past now. Her identical twin was gone, and she was alone in this world as she'd never been alone before.

Grant engulfed her in a big hug, and somehow

his compassion made her that much sadder. Poor Helena had missed so much. If only she could've seen Davin, just once, before the accident. Too many precious years had been wasted during their estrangement.

No sense pretending it was anything other than that. Helena had known her parents were finished with her. The pregnancy had been something they could never forgive. But she still could've come home to see Amalie and Davin. Or so Amalie had once thought.

But maybe Helena had sensed that Amalie didn't want her to come home. Maybe she'd known Amalie's deepest fear was that Helena would change her mind about Davin and take him away from her.

Legally, of course, Davin was Amalie's. But if Helena had wanted him, if her own twin sister had returned to claim her flesh-and-blood child, how could she have said no?

"It's been my fault all along." She hadn't meant to say the words, but they were true. If Helena had felt wanted at home, that was where she would have come. This accident never would have happened. Helena would still be alive.

"No, of course it isn't."

"I lived in fear of Helena coming home and taking Davin from me. She must have known that, Grant. That's why she never came back."

"You can't seriously blame yourself for loving Davin as your son."

Grant couldn't see it, of course. He thought Helena was all bad, Amalie all good. As if anything were ever that simple.

Still, he wouldn't let her go. Kissed the top of her head. The tip of her nose. "You're cold."

And he was warm. "You must think I'm crazy. A twenty-nine-year-old virgin with ESP." *Only, not a virgin anymore.*

"I'm a scientist, Amalie, but I know there are phenomena with no reasonable explanation. I don't think you're crazy."

"I've done some reading. Other identical twins have reported experiencing a similar ability to communicate across distance, just like my sister and me."

Grant squeezed her again.

"So what do we do now?" she asked.

"I want to conduct a few tests and take some measurements. But I have a hunch that everything's going to check out just fine. When we get back I'll organize a search party."

Grant's gaze connected with hers.

"We're going to find your sister."

THEY ARRIVED BACK in Revelstoke late Thursday evening. Grant helped carry her gear up to her apartment, then Amalie ran downstairs to Heidi's place. She was worried Davin might still be put out at having missed the chance for backcountry skiing. But when he greeted her at the door, he had a big smile.

"Mrs. Eitelbach is an awesome skier for an old lady," he said. "We went on this eight-mile trail, and she never got tired once. And she's almost as old as Grandma. Can you imagine Grandma doing that?"

Amalie couldn't.

"What trail was this?" she asked Heidi. She'd known they were planning to go skiing, but eight miles seemed long for the trails along the Summit Road.

Grant appeared behind her in time to hear Heidi's answer.

"Balu Pass Trail."

Amalie recognized the name and her protective instincts went on alert. "You went skiing in the mountains? Where is Balu Pass exactly? I can't remember."

She felt Grant's hand on her shoulder, a moment before she heard his answer. "The trailhead is at the Rogers Pass center, and the route follows between Mount Cheopps and Grizzly Mountain."

She turned back to Heidi. "I thought we agreed you'd stay close to town."

The landlady was unrepentant. "We were wearing transceivers and we checked with the warden's office before we left. The avalanche risk was classified as low.''

"Low. But there *was* a risk.''

"Balu Pass crosses several potential avalanche paths,'' Grant said. "But Heidi's right. The risk of avalanche in that corridor right now is minimal.''

Minimal was not the same as zero. Amalie felt physically sick at the idea of Davin skiing in any area that wasn't absolutely safe.

"I appreciate that you were willing to take Davin skiing, Heidi. But you were supposed to stick to the trails along Summit Road.''

"But those are so *boring*.''

Amalie put a hand on Davin's head. "I know, but you're a beginner.''

"He doesn't ski like a beginner,'' Heidi said bluntly. "You can't coddle a boy with Davin's energy,'' she said. "It only leads to more trouble in the end.''

"Avoiding avalanche territory doesn't necessarily equate with coddling, Heidi.''

"I see I've made you angry. I'm sorry about that. You're a good mother to Davin, and maybe I should have kept to the ski paths I knew you approved of. But Davin is growing up, Amalie. That's something you've got to remember.''

"Eleven is still a child. Not even a teenager,'' Amalie said.

"I'll be twelve in another month.''

"Yes. That's true." Amalie acknowledged Davin's desire to have his increasing maturity recognized. Ever since he'd learned to walk, she'd been trying to assure Davin's well-being, while not becoming like the overprotective parents her own mother and father had been.

Still, you'd think sticking to a safe cross-country trail wouldn't be too much to ask.

LATER THAT EVENING, while Davin was in the shower, Amalie dialed her parents' number. She didn't look forward to the conversation.

"We're getting by," her mother replied to Amalie's inquiry. "I finally hired that young Mackenzie boy down the street to clear the driveway for us. You know it's too much for your father—"

"How is Dad? Is his back any better?" Amalie tucked the phone under her ear as she measured flour for the muffins she was baking.

"Some. Not much. We were hoping you'd be back in time to drive us into Toronto for that appointment with the specialist."

"It doesn't look like I will." Both her parents could handle a car just fine. But they hated dealing with the traffic in Toronto. "Maybe you could park at one of the shopping malls and take a cab from there."

"A cab?" Her mother gave a sound of disbelief. "Do you have any idea what that would cost? Perhaps I should postpone the appointment until you return.''

"I'm not sure when that will be, Mom. Although I do think we'll be able to recover the bodies soon.'' Before her mother could comment on that, she interjected a question. "Did you know Helena was married?''

"Married?'' A moment of stunned silence followed. "To whom?''

"A man from Seattle named Matthew Stanway. He's planning to fly here when they've found—'' Amalie paused, swallowed. "Maybe you and Dad should come, too.''

"I don't see why. You're not expecting to find Helena alive, are you?''

Amalie set down the measuring cup and sank to the floor. Cross-legged, she leaned her head back against a cupboard door. "Of course not, Mom. That isn't the point.''

"Then what *is* the point? You've missed three weeks of work. And what about the boy? He ought to be in school.''

"Oh, Mom. Don't you want to know what happened to Helena? Don't you even care—''

"Of course I care. That doesn't mean I can't be practical. And I expect you to be the same. Generally, you are, although saddling yourself with that boy wasn't one of your shining moments.''

This was an old argument, but it still made Amalie burn with resentment. "Davin is your grand-child. How can you talk about him that way?"

"Because it wasn't supposed to happen this way, Amalie. We moved here so you and your sister could have the very best possible life. Raising an illegitimate child was *not* the plan."

"But Davin is—"

"Not only have you sacrificed your career, you've wasted your chances of finding a husband and having your own children because of him. I warned you there wasn't any man willing to take on the raising of a boy who wasn't his own. And I've been proven right, haven't I?"

"Davin is not the reason I haven't married." And even if he had been, he would have been worth the sacrifice.

From down the hallway, a door slammed. Davin must have finished his shower and gone to his room. Hopefully he hadn't heard—

"The truth is, Mother, my visits to see you and Dad every weekend cut down on more of my social opportunities than my responsibilities to Davin."

On the other end of the line, her mother's in-drawn breath was clearly audible. Amalie felt a flicker of regret. Lashing back was not the answer to dealing with her parents.

"Look, I'm sorry—"

"Never mind." The acid tone carried perfectly over the thousand miles of wire that separated them.

"You just get yourself back home. That's the main thing."

Amalie thought of Grant and his request that she move to Revelstoke. Not that it was something she was seriously considering. But for a moment she felt a vindictive urge to tell her mother she wasn't ever coming home again.

Of course she didn't. Her parents were stubborn and rigid, but they'd done their best by her.

"Goodbye, Mother. Give my love to Dad."

CHAPTER FIFTEEN

OVER THE NEXT FEW DAYS Grant spent hours with Ralph Carlson organizing the search party for Ramsey and Helena. Together they decided to send four men—there was going to be a lot of probing—plus a trained German shepherd, and his handler from Jasper. Ralph would oversee the operation from the warden's office at Rogers Pass, while Grant would lead the team of workers into the backcountry.

This was one operation where Grant definitely wanted a "hands-on" involvement. He'd been to the scene three times now—no one knew the terrain, or the dangers it presented, better than he did.

Besides, this was personal. Ramsey had been his best friend. As for Helen...well, she was Amalie's sister, and that would have been enough for him. But lately, he was aware that his anger and hostility toward the woman had been easing. She wasn't the first novice skier to be lured by the inviting promise of a pristine mountain bowl. As for the affair, Ramsey was a consenting adult. Grant couldn't really put all the blame on Helen.

Not that he expected Denise to be so forgiving.

Yesterday he'd put in a few more hours on her basement, sat through another Sunday meal, although he'd managed to leave before the kids were put to bed. While helping with dishes in the kitchen, though, he'd told her that they'd be going out to the accident site on Monday. He'd also told her the latest news about the affair.

He'd questioned Ramsey's colleagues at the hospital and at his practice, and none of them seemed to know anything about it.

Except one—

"What do you think, Boss?" A spray of snow had preceded the question as Peder skied to a stop just a foot in front of him, interrupting his musings.

"We'll have to do a little control work before we mark out the search area," he said.

Peder nodded, then went to get the handheld charges they would need.

Grant reached for his radio. He ought to check in with Ralph, but his thoughts were with Amalie. She and Davin were waiting in the safety of the Rogers Pass warden's office. Grant had spent most of the weekend with her and Davin, and knew that she was counting the minutes until they dragged her sister's body off this mountain. He only hoped they wouldn't disappoint her.

"THEY'RE ABOUT TO START control work," Ralph repeated, even though Amalie had heard the voice over the radio as clearly as he had.

Grant's voice. She hated to think of him up there, minutes away from skiing into the same avalanche territory that had taken her sister's life.

"Control work?" Davin was making notes for his research project. He'd bought a spiral notebook for this purpose and had taped a postcard view of Mount Tupper on the cover.

"Same principle as what you saw us doing with the howitzer last week," Ralph said. "They'll throw some handheld charges onto the slopes to release any unstable snow."

Amalie twisted in her chair to look out the window. As always, mountains obscured the horizon, this time the jagged outlines of the Sir Donald Range, and she felt the chest-tightening anxiety that she always experienced in their presence. She struggled to overcome her fear by saying a silent prayer for the men working in the shadow of those peaks.

"Boy, I wish I could see them throw in the bombs!" Davin pressed his nose to the glass.

"Oh, Davin." The mountains didn't intimidate him at all. Where did he find his courage?

Despite her own fear, though, she, too, wished she could be out on the slopes with the men. She ought to be present when they found Helena. *If* they found Helena. But Grant had been adamant that she stay behind.

"Do you think we'll hear the explosions?" Davin asked.

"I don't think so." Amalie wondered what it was about little boys and gunpowder. She'd never allowed violent toys or games in the house, yet this stuff just seemed to fascinate Davin.

"Would you like a refill?"

Ralph had slipped out to the coffee room. Now he offered up the glass carafe, only half-full, although they'd made a fresh pot just an hour ago.

"Thanks, Ralph." Amalie held up her foam cup, knowing she shouldn't. At this rate, she'd be a caffeine junkie before the mission was over. "Is the weather forecast still looking clear?"

A brief shadow crossed the park ranger's face. "A storm *is* blowing in. Seemed to come out of nowhere. At 5:30 this morning, there was no sign of it. But hopefully we'll be all finished before it hits."

"You've told Grant?"

Ralph nodded. "Don't worry about him. He knows what he's doing out there. He won't risk anybody getting hurt."

Not even himself?

That was when Amalie realized she was more worried about Grant than about whether they would find Helena. What had she been thinking, pressing for recovery of bodies when there was even the slightest chance that one of the men on the patrol might be hurt?

She pictured them now on the slopes she'd traversed with Grant only days ago. The snow had stabilized, Grant had said. That didn't mean there was no risk. If something happened to Grant—

Amalie truncated the thought, impatient at her own misplaced loyalties. Grant was a professional; he knew what he was doing. The reason she was here, after all, had nothing to do with him. She was here for her sister, because of the special bond between them and because of the son that they shared.

This trip was not supposed to be about meeting a man, about having her first sexual experience— although that had been incredible. She was in mourning for her sister—she couldn't be falling in love.

Except that she already had.

For a moment, Amalie entertained the notion of being married to Grant. She imagined watching him walk out the door morning after morning, knowing he was going to be putting his life on the line, and going through the suspense of wondering just how long his luck would hold out. Did the wives of the other men on his team ever get used to the dangers? She really didn't think she could.

IT WAS AN HOUR BEFORE SUNSET when they found the bodies. First Ramsey's; then, fifteen minutes later, Helena's. Back and shoulders aching from hours of prodding and shoveling, Grant called right away with the news.

"The coroner will be flying the bodies to Revelstoke," he said into the radio. The men were putting them into Jenny bags now.

Not a fun assignment. Both bodies had been encased in ice. Which was to be expected. A warm body melted the snow around it. After death, the body cooled quickly, and the melted snow froze into an ice coffin.

"No time to get the men off the mountain before dark."

He nodded, agreeing with Ralph's assessment. "We'll spend the night, then come down first thing in the morning. Have the coffee waiting, will you?"

He could picture Amalie hovering behind Ralph, those frown lines marring her forehead, but he didn't ask to speak with her. He was surprised, though, when her voice came over the radio next, instead of Ralph's.

"You're okay, Grant? All the men are okay?"

"Sure, Amalie." What was a little exhaustion, a few sore muscles, compared with what had happened to Ramsey and Helena?

Helping to carry two plastic-coated bodies into the helicopter wouldn't be the highlight of his career. The coroner had promised a copy of his report once it was filed. But Grant didn't need to read any such thing to know what had happened.

"I'd say Helena died from lack of oxygen. As you thought."

"What about Ramsey?"

"It looked like he suffered from trauma sustained during the avalanche." Most people underestimated the force of the snow as it pounded down the moun tain. For many unfortunate victims, this was the cause of death as they were plunged down cliffs, battered against trees, rocks.

Grant fought to control his voice. "He probably died within seconds."

"Oh, Grant."

There was nothing more to be said, really. At least it had been a speedy end.

"We'll be comfortable in the cabin where you and I—" Grant cut himself off. Cleared his throat. Continued. "Anyway, we'll be spending the night and returning in the morning."

"You're sure everyone's okay? Grant, you sound so worn-out."

"We're fine. Exhausted, but fine. See you to-morrow."

It took an effort of will for him to turn off the radio and to disconnect from Amalie. He knew she had more questions, and just hearing her voice had helped ease the emptiness he felt at his core. But he had to supervise cleanup of the search area. Finding bodies was messy business.

AMALIE BARELY SLEPT that night, thinking about her sister, about the life that had been far too short.

And worrying about Grant, out on that mountain for yet another night.

The next morning, she decided to go to the trailhead to greet him when he returned. She left Davin at home to work on his project under Heidi's supervision, and waited at the parking lot just off the highway.

Overnight, the storm had settled in—another factor that had increased her concern. Unable to sit still in her warm car, Amalie paced outside in the snow, stamping her feet and holding a mitten to her mouth to keep the frost from her lungs. Fat flakes of snow were falling, covering the shoulders of her suede jacket as quickly as she could brush them off.

Snow. More depressing snow. Along the Rogers Pass it just accumulated from one storm to the next. She had no way of knowing if it was causing problems for the men out on the mountain. Maybe she should have gone to the warden's office, instead of waiting on her own.

A distant rumble warned of an approaching vehicle. Through the veil of snowflakes, Amalie watched as a sturdy Jeep pulled up next to her Jetta. Then she was distracted by sounds from the forest in front of her. When she sighted the familiar blue anoraks, she cried out in relief.

''There they are!''

Grant was in the lead, easy to pick out with his height and breadth. He saw her, too, and raised his ski pole in salute. Pushing through fresh drifts of snow, she moved toward him, suspecting she was foolish for feeling this wild, heady relief, but unable to stop herself.

He looked a little tired, but otherwise it was Grant as usual. Not even out of breath from the early-morning tour.

"You *are* fine?" She reached out and her mitten rasped against his unshaven beard. He didn't seem embarrassed by her behavior. In fact, he scooped her into his arms and kissed her. Right in front of all his men.

Someone whistled. Good-naturedly, Grant waved them forward. "Go home and say hello to your own women. And enjoy the break, because with all this snow coming, we're going to be busy in the next few days."

Amalie laughed and leaned up to kiss him again. His lips and cheeks were stiff and cold, and she was determined to revive them.

"How bloody touching."

Denise's voice had Amalie whipping around to face her. Arms crossed, the woman stood by her Jeep, her face a mask of implacable fury.

"Obviously, the Fremont sisters are too much temptation for any man to resist. Full marks to you, Amalie. At least you picked a man who wasn't married."

The slur to her sister—whose body even now

was sitting in the morgue of the Revelstoke hospital—was malicious. Amalie had no urge to retaliate, however; this woman's husband was also lying there.

Grant pushed forward on his skis, traversing the short distance between him and Denise, leaving Amalie to follow in his tracks.

"Denise, I know how devastating this has been. But it isn't fair to blame Amalie for something her sister did. And face it, something Ramsey did, too."

That was the first time he hadn't placed all the blame squarely on Helena's shoulders, and Amalie felt another rush of warmth toward this man who'd just returned from such a thankless mission.

"You've got to come to terms with this, Denise." Grant was close enough now to reach out a kind hand, but Ramsey's widow jerked away from his touch. "I was hoping that finding the bodies would bring you some peace."

"Peace?" Denise's usually pretty features were transformed by the slash of bleak lines across her forehead and down either side of her small mouth. "I'll never feel at peace about Ramsey's death."

She turned her eyes, darkened with misery, toward Amalie. "And I'll never forgive you or your sister for being the cause of it. As for Grant—"

She swung back to him, her voice raising. "You were supposed to be Ramsey's best friend. My

friend, too…'' Her voice became choked with emo-
tion, then she gained control. ''But you certainly
were quick to fall into this woman's arms.'' She
yanked on the door to the Jeep, once more pushing
Grant aside.

''You think she's so different from her sister?''
Denise's words dripped with venomous intent.
''They're identical twins, for God's sake. How dif-
ferent can they be?''

IDENTICAL TWINS. The words rang in Amalie's ears
as she drove back to the apartment, with Grant following in his truck.

The circumstances of birth had made life complicated for Amalie and her sister. Still, this was the
first time she'd heard the relationship ''identical
twins'' referred to as some kind of curse.

And here in Revelstoke that was exactly what it
felt like. All because of the terrible reputation her
sister had earned in two short months. Amalie
wished she could understand how this was possible.
For her sister to have changed so much, something
must have happened. What could it have been?

Maybe Helena's husband, Matthew, would be
able to answer that question. They were expecting
him early this afternoon—assuming the snowstorm
didn't hold him up.

What would he be like, this husband Helena had
never bothered to mention? On the phone he'd

sounded kind, polite. Amalie had called him last night to report that the bodies had been found. He'd been stunned by the news, as if he'd harbored a secret hope that the whole misadventure would prove a mistake.

But yesterday had dispelled even that faint hope. Helena and Ramsey had been together on that mountain. Two married people who had no business being alone together in the first place. And now they were dead.

It was a high price to pay for infidelity.

"DENISE CARTER IS just jealous," Heidi Eitelbach pronounced some hours later, after hearing a watered-down version of the confrontation by the highway.

She'd made hot chocolate for all of them. Grant, Amalie, Davin and herself. And for the newcomer. Helena's husband, Matthew Stanway.

Matthew had arrived an hour ago. He'd phoned from a service station by the highway, where he was having his flashy black Jaguar fitted with snow chains.

"The RCMP pulled me over for speeding." He'd sounded aggrieved. "Then they told me my tires weren't safe for winter driving in the mountains."

"I'll come get you," Amalie promised. After hanging up, she relayed the story to the others. They'd all laughed, even Davin.

She'd refused Grant's offer to accompany her and set out for the service station feeling slightly apprehensive. So much of what she'd learned about Helena thus far had been disappointing. She was afraid Matthew Stanway would be, too.

Extremely tall, extremely slender, with wavy light-brown hair and a wide, generous mouth, Matthew hadn't needed an Armani suit and white wool overcoat to stand out in the small family restaurant that was attached to the service station.

He stared the moment he set eyes on Amalie, and that was when she'd known Helena hadn't told him that she had an identical twin. Swallowing the pain, Amalie held out her hand and told Matthew her name.

He ignored the hand, engulfed her in a big hug, then promptly broke down into tears.

Amalie had liked him immediately. "Lucky you made it here before the storm got much worse," she said as they walked past his car and she had a chance to see the fine tread on his tires. He would have skimmed over the icy highways like a cat on roller blades.

"This storm is going to get worse?" Matthew walked with his upper body bent forward about twenty degrees, shielding his face from the bitter wind.

"Afraid so." Amalie had smiled, watching him fold his legs inside the front seat of her Jetta. Driving back to Helena's apartment, she sounded him out to see what else he didn't know.

"Helena's son is here, too," she'd started.

Matthew's blank look had confirmed that Helena had kept other secrets, as well.

"Davin is eleven," she'd explained as she drove. "I've raised him since he was a baby."

"Helena never visited." This was a statement, not a question.

"No." Amalie glanced at the tall man for a moment and noted his thoughtful expression.

"Hmm," was all he said.

Once inside Heidi's apartment, Amalie had made introductions and Matthew had shaken the land-lady's hand graciously, then bent on one knee to regard Davin. Finally he stood again and thanked Grant for his part in finding Helena's body.

"I'd like to have a memorial service for Helena at home in Seattle, where our friends are," he said. Then he looked at Amalie. "If that's okay with you."

Amalie nodded, relieved that Matthew appeared to be a gentle-mannered and considerate person. And she agreed with his decision. She didn't want the service to take place in Revelstoke, where Helena had acted with such confusing indiscretion. Nor did she think it was necessary to ask for the service to be held back home. If her parents had truly cared, they'd be here right now.

To acknowledge that her parents hadn't cared—not about Davin and now not about her sister, either—was painful.

"This hot chocolate is like nothing I've ever tasted." Matthew was sipping his with the appreciation of a gourmet.

"Real Swiss chocolate. And none of that low-fat milk nutritionists are always pushing down our throats." Heidi raised her eyebrows at Amalie.

"Of course Denise was jealous," Grant said, returning to the original thread of the conversation. "Of Helen." He shot an embarrassed look at Matthew, then continued. "But why lash out at Amalie?"

"At that moment it *was* Amalie she was jealous of." Heidi scooped the last mound of whipped cream onto her hot of chocolate. "Davin, would you be a dear and run to the corner store to get me another carton?" She passed him a handful of change.

When he was gone, the older lady turned back to Grant. "Ever since Ramsey's death she's been leaning on you, and you've been too much of a gentleman to see what's going on."

"Come on, now." Grant's cheeks turned ruddy. "Her husband's just died."

"So? You think it hasn't happened before? A woman turning to another man after the death of her husband?"

"I'm not following," Matthew cut in politely. "What does Helena have to do with this Denise?"

Amalie looked to Grant, who gave her a slight nod. "I'm afraid you haven't been filled in on all the circumstances of Helena's death." Quickly Amalie explained about the man who'd perished at Helena's side. The man who'd been having an affair with Matthew's wife.

"No." Matthew was shaking his head. "This is not Helena. I can't believe it." He stared at the fourth finger of his left hand, at his orange-gold ring with a sparkle of diamond chips across the face. Amalie remembered seeing a feminine counterpart in Helena's jewelry drawer. "We were everything to each other. Everything."

The sincerity in his words made Amalie want so desperately to believe him. This woman who'd stayed in Revelstoke for two months wasn't the Helena either of them had known. There'd been some mistake.

Yet now that the body had been found, there was no chance of that. Amalie couldn't understand it. Nothing made sense.

Grant was openly skeptical. "If your marriage was so perfect, why did your wife leave you?" The question was blunt, but there was compassion in his face as he waited for Matthew's reply.

When it came, none of them was ready.

"I don't know the full answer to that question,"

Matthew said. "But I know it had something to do with Helena's pregnancy."

Amalie started. "You mean eleven years ago? When she had Davin?"

"No." Matthew gave her a small smile, full of misgiving and sorrow. "The baby she was due to have in July. The baby she found out about the day before she left me."

CHAPTER SIXTEEN

DAVIN HELD THE FRONT DOOR ajar with one hand and squeezed the carton of cream with his other. Holy cow! Helena had been pregnant?

If she'd lived, maybe she'd have given the new baby to Aunt Amalie, too. He could've had a brother or sister!

Or maybe she would have kept this baby. The thought made him feel as though something black, thick and poisonous had spilled inside his chest. He closed the door softly and stood where no one would see him, with his back pressed against the wall that separated the kitchen from the hall. If they knew he was here they'd stop talking; then he'd never find out anything.

"But Helena couldn't have another baby," Aunt Amalie was saying.

"Why not?" Helena's husband asked.

"After Davin's birth Helena was warned not to get pregnant again. I thought she was going to have her tubes tied. Obviously, she didn't."

Tubes tied? That was a puzzler. But the part that really had him curious was that statement about his birth. Why no more babies? Didn't most women have more than one kid once they got started?

"Tell me, Amalie." It was Matthew again. "What happened when Davin was born?"

"Oh, it was awful. I can't remember the medical terms, but I know the complications were very rare and very serious. At one point her heart actually stopped beating and she had to be resuscitated. We were so afraid she was going to die."

Davin hadn't realized it was possible to die just from having a baby. That old sick feeling churned up in his stomach. He forced himself to keep listening.

"Hours after the delivery Helena began hemorrhaging. You can't imagine how frightful it was— the blood came from every orifice. Her eyes, her ears, the insertion point for her intravenous..."

It was like a horror movie. Davin could picture a lady who looked like his aunt rising up from bed, blood spurting from her head and arms, reaching with menacing hands for the baby who had caused so much trouble.

Suddenly a whole lot of things made sense. That was why his mother had run away. He'd hurt her so bad. He'd almost killed her.

He heard a faint thud, glanced down and saw the container of whipping cream on the floor. He bent over, was about to pick it up, when another thought struck him.

Did Aunt Amalie blame him for what happened to her sister?

His grandparents' faces loomed in his consciousness. They blamed him, too. Because of him one daughter had almost died and their other daughter wasn't able to get married.

Because no man would want to be *his* father.

All of a sudden so many things made sense. About the past, about his family. Oddly enough, the world he was in right now had gone strangely blurry. Davin reached a hand to his eyes and felt wetness.

Gosh, he was crying like a baby. He couldn't let anyone see him. But he didn't want to go up to Helena's apartment.

He needed to get away. Somewhere far away so he could have time to think.

Davin groped for the door handle, then carefully closed it behind him as he left.

"WHAT WAS THAT SOUND?" Amalie went out into the hall, where she was certain she'd heard someone come in. But the door was shut; all was normal. Only...

On the floor was a slightly squashed container of whipping cream. She picked it up and carried it to the fridge.

"Davin, are you in here?"

"Maybe he went back to your apartment," Heidi suggested. "To sneak in a little television."

"I suppose. I gave him a key when we went on that ski trip." He should have checked in, though. And it had been careless to leave the cream on the floor that way. But she would talk to him about it later.

Right now she needed to find out about Helena and Matthew. This pregnancy, she was sure, was the key to everything. "You had no idea how dangerous childbirth would have been to Helena?"

He shook his head, face covered by his hands. After a few moments, he peered out from between long fingers and sighed heavily. "She told me she wanted to terminate the pregnancy. I couldn't understand why. She never explained—" His breath broke on a ragged sob. "I just thought she was frightened. Helena was timid about a lot of things."

Amalie looked automatically to Grant. The rough-edged mountaineer appeared completely befuddled. She supposed none of this sounded like the Helena he'd thought he'd known.

"If only she'd told me. I wanted our baby, but I would never have put her at any risk...."

"What did you say when she wanted to terminate the pregnancy?" Amalie asked.

"I told her she was being silly." His regret was obvious as he brushed his hands up and down the

length of his face. "But she'd never said anything... I didn't know...."

"And so she took off." Amalie thought of that
fissure of despair she'd felt in mid-December. That
had to be it. Helena finding out she was pregnant.
Helena leaving impulsively in her luxury coupe, no
real plans, no thought to the future.

*Maybe some vague idea about returning to On-
tario to see her family. Plans thwarted by something as mundane as having the incorrect tires for
her car. It was possible.*

"Once she made the decision to stay in Revelstoke, I'm surprised she didn't go to a doctor," she
said, trying to put herself in her sister's shoes.
"With her medical history there would have been
no problem arranging to terminate the pregnancy."

Grant's face went white. Amalie reached out a
hand, squeezed his fingers. "Are you okay?"

He gave her a look, like she was missing something.

"Grant? What is it?"

"Ramsey." He choked out the name. "Ramsey
was a doctor. He could have performed the abortion
for her."

THE LAST THING Grant had ever expected was to
feel sorry for Helena Fremont. He did now.

Inspecting the people gathered around the
kitchen table, he saw Amalie, Heidi and Matthew

all watching him expectantly. Ironic how the research he'd thought he'd been doing on Denise's behalf should turn out to be so helpful now. But Matthew wouldn't know about that.

"Ramsey Carter's widow asked me to see if I could find out how long her husband had been having an affair with—with your wife."

Matthew looked at him impassively. Clearly, he still didn't believe Helena would do such a thing. And Grant was beginning to think he might be right.

"A friend of mine had seen them at a restaurant about a week before the accident. They were having what appeared to be a serious conversation. Helena was crying."

Amalie leaned forward eagerly. "They could have been discussing the abortion."

Now Matthew nodded. "That would make sense."

"I also talked with some people at the hospital and at Ramsey's private practice. Off-the-record, you understand."

This time everyone nodded.

"His receptionist told me Helena had made an appointment to see Ramsey about ten days before the accident. As far as I can tell, that was the first time they met."

"So Helena and Ramsey weren't having an af

fair." Amalie sounded triumphant. "He was her doctor, and she was trying to arrange an abortion."

She sounded so relieved Grant hated to point out the obvious. "Yes, but doctors don't usually take their patients on overnight skiing trips."

"Oh." Amalie's face fell.

"There has to be an explanation." Matthew's faith, it appeared, was not so easily shattered. "Perhaps Helena was having difficulty coming to terms with the actual abortion. Maybe the decision wasn't as simple as she'd expected it to be."

"I can't imagine it being an easy choice for any woman," Amalie said. "Our parents are vigorously opposed to abortion on any grounds. Perhaps their opinions, and that of our church, held more sway with Helena than she realized."

"Still..." It seemed he was doomed to play the role of the skeptic. "Wouldn't the logical thing be for Ramsey to arrange counseling for her?"

"Maybe he was. In a way." Amalie laid a fine-boned hand out on the table. "Didn't Denise Carter tell you Ramsey proposed to her out at that cabin?"

At first Grant didn't see. Then he recalled more of the conversation. "That's right. Apparently, Ramsey always made that particular trek when he had an important decision at hand."

Would Ramsey take a confused patient out to the Asulkan Hut to help her come to terms with her decision? Maybe it was a little far-fetched, but overall, Grant felt it fit with his view of Ramsey's character a lot more than the notion of him having a fling

Plus, as Amalie had pointed out earlier, the Asulkan Hut was not exactly the most comfortable spot, if sex was your only object.

"I'm going to make more hot chocolate," Heidi announced, rising from the table. "Everyone?"

They all nodded. Amalie decided to run up to her apartment to see if Davin wanted more, too.

"Although I'm sure he'll say yes."

The mood around the table had lightened considerably, now that this new explanation for Helena and Ramsey's expedition had been unearthed. Grant wondered if they'd ever be able to prove it, and whether it would provide Denise with the peace she was looking for.

Certainly, it eased his own confused feelings about Ramsey's death.

"The more I think about it," Matthew said, "the more it makes sense. Helena had a terrible time coming to decisions. And she would have had no one in Revelstoke to help her with this one."

He rose to pace the small kitchen, his narrow shoulders hunched beneath the stiff cotton of his shirt.

Poor man, Grant thought. These past few months couldn't have been easy on him. His love for Helena appeared to be genuine. For the first time, Grant could see how a man might love Helena.

But not him. She had been too flighty. In this respect, at least, she was her sister's opposite. Amalie didn't see herself as brave, but she faced her problems head-on. It was one of many things he admired about her.

The aroma of Heidi's warming chocolate made his stomach gurgle, reminding him he hadn't had lunch.

"I don't know about the rest of you," he said, "but I'm starved. How about I order in a couple of pizzas?"

Both Heidi and Matthew seemed to think this was a good suggestion. He picked up the phone and was soon talking to Blaine.

"Keeping busy?"

"Lots of delivery business with this snow. Don't suppose it'll hold up the damn franchise inspector, though. Expect him in a day or two, but other than that, everything's peachy. What can I get for you?"

Halfway through the order, the apartment door swung open. Amalie burst into the room, obviously panicked.

"Davin isn't in the apartment. And his ski equipment is missing."

He dropped the phone as she turned to him.

"Oh, Grant! It's going to be dark soon. Surely he hasn't gone skiing."

For a moment he stared at the others in shocked silence. Then it seemed as if everyone began talking at once.

"We have to—"

"Do you think—"

"I hope he didn't—"

"Please, everyone." Grant held up his hands, trying to achieve calm, the preliminary step in any emergency situation.

"We have to think this through. First, what time did you find that carton of cream on the floor, Amalie?"

"I can't remember!" Amalie had her hand to her throat. She'd moved to the window, and Grant knew what she was doing. Staring at those mountains, cursing those mountains. Now she had one more reason to resent the landscape he would always consider home.

"It was past three when I sent him for the cream," Heidi said. "I remember the cuckoo went just before I handed Davin the change."

Heidi's Swiss clock hung above the kitchen table. They all stared at it now, and, as if on cue, the long hand reached out to twelve, the door slid open, a small bird popped out. One, two, three, four times.

Grant figured the boy had thirty minutes, maybe forty-five, on them.

"I'm going to call the RCMP. There's no way Davin would make it far without hitching a ride.

Meanwhile, we'd better break into two groups. Heidi, you stay here at home base with Amalie.''

"Stay?" Amalie practically charged him. "No way, Grant. I'm coming with you. I just *know* he's headed for the ski trails.''

"Which narrows down the search," Grant said, agreeing with her. "Davin is only familiar with two sets of cross-country trails. The ones along Summit Road—" which would be safe, even in this weather.

"And the Balu Pass Trail." Heidi held her head in her hands, as if she wished she could tear it from her shoulders. "You were right, Amalie. I was foolish to take him there. So foolish.''

Amalie touched the woman's shoulder. "Don't blame yourself, Heidi. No one could have known he would do something like this. He's never gone off without asking me first. Perhaps the strain of the past few days has been too much…maybe he harbored a secret hope that we would find his mother—alive.''

"Or maybe he overheard our conversation," Matthew suggested. "How much of that old history was he aware of? That Helena almost died in childbirth, for instance.''

Amalie shook her head. "I never told him. I didn't want him to think he was in any way responsible." A new terror widened her eyes. She reached out for Grant. "Oh, no, what have I done?''

"Don't worry. We'll find him." Quickly Grant recalculated the rescue mission. "Matthew, you stay at Helena's apartment. Heidi, you stay here. Do you have a cell phone, Matthew?"

"Yes."

"Okay, Heidi, use that to call everyone you know, especially people Davin might have met. Leave the main line clear in case he decides to phone home."

He grabbed his jacket, made sure his cell phone was turned on.

"Let's go, Amalie. We'll call the RCMP from my car."

Grant loaded Amalie's ski equipment onto his truck, where his own gear was still unpacked from his morning trip. Fatigue was forgotten as Grant turned the truck up the Trans-Canada toward the Rogers Pass Information Center.

First he called the highway patrol division to have them watch out for a young hitchhiker, then the warden's office, where he asked if some men could check out the Summit Trails.

"I'm on my way to Balu Pass," he said into the radio. Sensing Amalie's terror, he added, "With his mother. We think he might be headed there. If I see any sign of him, I'll let you know. "

If they were lucky.

"Maybe he's not headed for a ski trail at all. Maybe he just…" But what other explanation could there be? He'd taken his equipment. Surely, though, he had more sense than to go off on a trail when it would soon be dark. It was nearing mid-February, so the sun would be setting shortly after five.

"If he heard what we were saying, he must be so upset. He won't be thinking rationally, Grant. Who knows what he might do. He might get himself lost...."

Amalie herself sounded lost. He covered her hand and tried to offer hope. "If he has, we'll find him. The RCMP are looking, my guys have the Summit Trails covered..."

And that left Balu Pass to them. And about fifty-five minutes of remaining daylight.

AMALIE WAS TRYING HARD not to panic and not to cry. Neither would help in finding Davin and they had to make the most of their precious remaining minutes of daylight. She had her skis on and was ready to go. Anxiously, she looked at Grant.

"Do you have a beeper?" he asked.

She held up her transceiver and he nodded approval.

Thank God for Grant. Practical, yes, but also knowledgeable, skilled, strong...a veritable warrior on skis. If anyone could find Davin, he could.

A radio call from a local RCMP constable ten minutes earlier had confirmed that a trucker had picked up a young boy at about three-thirty. The boy said he'd been separated from his school group and asked to be dropped off at the hotel by the information center.

The slickness of the lie stunned Amalie. Immediately, Grant had called off the search at Summit Road and radioed the guys at the warden's office for backup, while Amalie ran inside the hotel to see if Davin had been there.

He hadn't.

Searchers would be arriving in ten minutes, but Grant said they couldn't wait, and Amalie agreed. At present Davin's tracks were visible on the gently ascending path. But with the steady falling snow and the fading light, they soon wouldn't be.

"We'll catch him, Amalie. He doesn't have much on us." Grant led the way, not even looking back, as if assuming that she'd be able to keep up.

And she did. Amalie hadn't known she could move with such speed. No short easy strides this time. Instead, she pushed off with each stroke, and was surprised how much farther and faster her skis took her. Maybe the trip last week had toughened her, conditioned her.

After a few minutes, the trees were so thick on either side of her that she felt as though she was traveling through a tunnel. Her legs working at a running pace, she practically flew along the trail. She was moving so fast that she ran into Grant's skis when he stopped to check on her.

"Sorry..."

"It looks like he's branched off the main trail here."

He pointed to the ski path that veered off at a right angle. "This is known as the Hourglass. It's a fun little trail during normal ski conditions."

Amalie heard the big "but" implicit in his sentence. These weren't normal ski conditions. The early-morning storm had changed everything, plus the temperature was warmer now than it had been for several days. Even she knew that was a dangerous indicator for avalanches.

"Make sure you keep well behind me, Amalie. If something does happen—the most important thing will be to recall the last point you saw me or Davin. Remember, the other guys are just minutes behind us at this point."

Amalie nodded. "Yes, I know. Let's get going."

A touch of a smile, then a nod. "That's the spirit." And he was off.

Even faster now, but he had to be. And so did she. It was ten minutes to five. Oh, God, they had fifteen more minutes of daylight, maximum. *Move, Amalie, move!*

She went around a curve, and the trees seemed to lean in toward her. Choking back fear, she kept her gaze focused on the ground before her skis. *Fly! Fly!* The very snow was scratching out the word as she moved, so quickly it was as if her feet had disconnected from the ground and she was skimming through the air.

Another curve, and Amalie caught a magnificent view of the towering Grizzly Mountains to the northwest. She felt their malevolent spirit rise up against hers, and struggled not to be cowed.

No! I will not give up.

Grant was so far ahead now she could see only the blue of his jacket. Then the path straightened briefly and she caught the most wonderful sight of her life—a flash of fluorescent yellow.

Davin.

Oh, thank you, Lord. Thank you. In his black-and-yellow high-tech ski jacket, Davin was skiing with all his might away from them.

"Davin!" She heard Grant call, too. Miraculously, the boy paused and glanced back at them.

Just as he raised his pole in acknowledgment, a rumble came from the mountain, a sound Amalie was all too familiar with after having watched avalanche control on the Rogers Pass.

She looked up. A light powder was rising from midway up the slope. As clearly as if a giant had taken a carving knife to it, she saw a slab of snow separate and begin to move downward.

At first it didn't appear dangerous. But within seconds the air was filled with the thunder of moving snow. The very ground trembled.

Davin! This time her cry was silent as she

watched the slab advance toward her son. He didn't even know what hit him, as it caught him from behind, burying him along with her heart.

No. Oh, no.

Amalie knew she had to mark the spot she'd last seen him and she fixed on a twisted pine tree that looked like a witch's peaked cap—she would remember that.

She started skiing forward again, frustrated when the volume of snow in the air made it difficult to see. The blue of Grant's coat became her target. She was concentrating so hard she forgot to leave time or space for stopping, and collided once more into the back of his skis.

"Grant—I saw Davin—it was by that tree." She raised a ski pole. God, seconds were ticking. Why wasn't he moving?

Davin was buried under all that snow. Could he breathe? Had he remembered to release his skis, drop his poles? Had there been time for him to react—everything had happened so fast.

"Amalie." Grant grasped her arm, his voice firm yet calm. He was staring up at the mountain, and finally she followed his gaze. The snow was still moving.

"We have to wait for this to stabilize."

"But—"

He gave her arm a yank. "We won't save him if we're buried ourselves. Here, take this radio. Talk the guys in. Tell them what to expect. As soon as it seems safe, I'm going to check for a reading from Davin's transceiver. Hopefully he was wearing one.''

Amalie hadn't noticed whether it was missing when she'd checked the apartment. ''I want to help.''

''You *will* help. By standing here.'' Grant pointed once more to the slope that had just released so much snow. ''That could go again and I'd be buried. Then you'll be our only hope.''

God, no. Not Grant, too. Not both of them. She couldn't stand it... Resolutely, she held in her terror. ''I understand.''

''Good. I'm going in now. If you have to move, do it slowly.''

Slowly. Yes. She raised the radio to her mouth, seeking contact with the men behind her. The men who worked, with Grant, on avalanche control...as if there were any such thing.

CHAPTER SEVENTEEN

IT WAS NOW FIVE O'CLOCK exactly, and although the sun had not yet set, it had disappeared behind the western range. Soon, very soon, it would be dark. Amalie gripped her flashlight with one hand, the radio with the other.

Talking to these men was the only way she could hold on to sanity when her every instinct urged her to ski down into the valley with Grant and help search for her son.

"Grant's got an area marked off. He's trying to pick up a signal."

Please be wearing your avalanche beacon, Davin. Amalie closed her eyes, remembering how she had felt when her sister had been swept under. The terrible pressure on her lungs and the resulting blind panic. *Conserve your energy,* she implored silently. *Don't struggle. Don't try to call out.* Because chances were no one would hear him anyway.

That was what Grant had told them. When you were buried under snow you could often hear movement from above, but efforts to call out were futile and only wasted precious oxygen.

Amalie turned back to the trail, looking for signs of the avalanche control team. If they didn't get here soon, she was going to go help Grant anyway. This standing around doing nothing—she couldn't take it.

Finally, she saw them. She had to wait only a minute or two, but sixty seconds was a long time to do nothing when someone you loved was in danger. She kept holding her breath, imagining Davin doing without oxygen for an equal length of time. They had to get him out!

When she was sure the men had seen her, she pointed her skis toward the crooked pine tree and flew, tucking her body low to keep her balance. Wind whooshed around her face as she swung over toward Grant. She was alarmed to see him toss the transceiver aside.

"I'm not picking up any signal. We'll have to start probing."

Amalie swallowed panic and glanced down at her watch. Almost three minutes had passed now. They were losing precious time. "The men are here."

"Good. It's important to be fast, but we also have to be methodical." Grant had his pack open and was piecing together an aluminum probe.

Amalie didn't have any official equipment, but she could use her pole. "I want to look by that tree."

Technique forgotten, she tucked over her skis

and let gravity take her forward. Several bumps almost threw her, then she fell on her side to stop herself. Here. This was where she'd last seen him. Turning on the flashlight, she searched for any sign at all. A glove, a ski tip...

Or a ski pole! She caught the black of the protruding handle in the glare of light.

"Grant! I see a pole! I think it's Davin's!"

In seconds he was there, then Peder and another man from the team. They pulled large shovels from their pack and worked like crazy men.

"Call for the helicopter ambulance, Amalie," Grant said between huffs. "When we find him he'll need immediate medical attention. We'll have to fly him to Revelstoke."

When we find him. Not *if* we find him. Amalie clung to this hope, refusing to believe the ski pole could belong to anyone but Davin.

Although the snow had just fallen, it was packed tight. As the pit the men were digging widened and deepened, they began to position their shovels more carefully.

"You're going to be okay, Davin." Grant had been talking the whole time. "We're digging you out right now. It'll only be a few minutes."

"Hang in there, baby," Amalie added, praying that her son could hear them. "I love you, Davin. Just another minute, I promise."

Another minute. A glance at her watch confirmed

that five minutes had passed since Davin had been swallowed up by the mountain's eruption.

How was it possible for so much to happen in so little time? Thank God they'd found him swiftly. Yet five minutes was a long time to go without air. Unless he'd been buried with a small pocket of precious oxygen...

These thoughts and more raced through Amalie's head. Again she thought of Helena, who hadn't been fortunate enough to have the avalanche control team on site within moments of her accident.

"I feel his hat...."

Shovels were tossed aside. Now the priority was to clear the area around his head. Bare hands were required. Amalie dropped to her knees and pushed and scraped at the snow, too.

Release him, you damn mountain!

Quickly his head was uncovered. Davin was unconscious, his skin blue.

God, no, they were too late...

But Grant was far from giving up. With his fingers he plucked the plugs of snow from Davin's mouth, his nostrils, and began mouth-to-mouth resuscitation. It only took a few breaths.

"He's breathing!" Grant announced. "But still unconscious, I think. Let's get him out of there, boys."

In a flurry of arms and flying snow, Davin's entire body was revealed, like a sculpture from a block of ice. The light in Amalie's hand wavered as a violent case of trembles overtook her.

Relief. Her boy was alive.

The thrumming of propellers, the roar of an engine and bright lights from above announced the arrival of the helicopter ambulance. Amalie was barely aware of it. She was completely focused on Davin, watching for any sign that he might be gaining consciousness.

Cautiously, limbs were tested for fracture.

"Careful with the left arm," Grant said. "I think we'll need a splint."

He'd broken his arm. Amalie decided she could live with that. *Please, Lord, let that be his only injury....*

The paramedic who had arrived from the helicopter, took Davin's vital signs, then he helped Grant splint the arm.

"Not bad, but let's put him on oxygen to be safe."

Within seconds, he was encased in a warm sleeping bag, then laid out on a backboard, a C-collar holding his neck and spine immobile.

"It's okay, Amalie. He's going to be fine."

Only then did she realize she was crying. Grant pulled her into his chest, and she could feel that he, too, was shaking. "That was one of the quickest rescue missions I've ever seen. Thank God you spotted that ski pole!"

AMALIE SAT BY DAVIN'S HOSPITAL BED, holding the hand of his unbroken arm, resting her face on the pillow next to his.

Grant had stayed on the mountain with his men, while she'd flown in the 'copter with Davin to the hospital. A broken arm was Davin's only injury. Already it was in a cast.

She supposed she'd been lucky. This was the first time she'd ended up in Emergency with her son, whereas most of her contemporaries were pros at the routine. What Davin lacked in frequency, however, he certainly compensated for with high drama!

GRANT PAUSED AT THE DOOR to the hospital room. Amalie was sleeping, her head next to Davin's. It was quite a sight. Those two blondies next to each other like that.

The fear he'd felt on the mountain came back to him, and he pressed his lips together and forced air up through his nostrils.

If anything had happened to that kid, he'd probably have fallen apart. And he never would've been able to face Amalie. She'd trusted him to save her son.

Thank God they had.

He took a few steps into the room, still staring at them, barely able to accept that they truly were safe. Hard to believe how much they'd come to mean to him in such a short time. He'd never had a craving for kids, but Davin… Something about the boy made him feel he might have a calling as a father yet.

As for Amalie, he couldn't live without her. He'd realized it as he watched her disappear into the sky in the helicopter. The flight hadn't been without risk. Low-lying clouds, the fading light… Grant had felt helpless as they'd left, aware that they were no longer in his care. It wasn't a feeling he was used to.

Nor was loving someone that much. Funny, he'd always thought that the woman he'd want to marry would be more like him, like his mother: sports-minded and adventurous. But those outer qualities weren't what counted. Amalie had courage, and determination, and a heart that reached out to people. In the end, that was all he wanted.

He took a few more steps, then sat in the chair next to Amalie's. He'd move to Ontario, if that would convince her of his love. There were national parks in that province, too. Somehow they'd come to a compromise if being close to her parents was so important to her.

Gently, he picked up a spare blanket and spread it over her back, then tucked the edge up under her chin. He didn't want to wake her, but he sure wished he could hold her in his arms for a few minutes.

AMALIE FELT THE BLANKET settle over her shoulders.

"Hey, there." She smiled, then smoothed her hair back from her face.

"He's okay?" Grant brushed her cheek with his lips, then pressed a hand to Davin's forehead.

"Yes, he's okay. Thanks to you." Amalie wondered how she could possibly repay a debt like this. And how a man could continually put his own life on the line for the sake of others, the way Grant did. She had no doubt that if Davin had been a stranger, Grant wouldn't have acted any differently. It was more than his job. It was *him.*

"Well, it was a real team effort, Amalie. And let's face it. We had luck—or something a little stronger—on our side."

She reached out for his hand and squeezed it. "Have you had a chance to call Heidi and Matthew?"

"Yes." He sat in the chair beside hers, not releasing her hand. "They wanted to come to the hospital right away, but I convinced them to wait until morning."

"Good."

"Amalie?"

"Yes?"

"Your sister…I was wrong about her, and I owe you an apology. I blamed her for Ramsey's death, and that wasn't right. Maybe she made the decision to ski into that bowl, but he shouldn't have taken her up there in the first place."

"Thank you." She wasn't sure why his opinion about Helena mattered, but it did. It always had.

"I was wrong about her, period, I guess. I was put off from the beginning because I thought there was something artificial about her. And there was— just too bad I never thought to wonder what she was trying so hard to hide from."

"Her fear. Grant, she was so alone."

"Ramsey was a good man. I feel certain he was trying to help her."

Knowing there'd been someone for Helena to talk to, to lean on, was a comfort. If the avalanche hadn't happened, would she have come off that mountain with the strength to terminate her pregnancy? Would she have gone back to Matthew? Maybe even come home one day, at least for a visit?

All questions that would never be answered.

"I'm glad you see her for what she was, Grant. That's important to me." More important than he could possibly understand. Even though she'd been apart from Helena for eleven years, she still had a sense of shared identity. She'd never been able to explain it. But it made it impossible for her to believe that anyone who despised her sister could love her, Amalie.

For all their differences, they still had too much in common.

Like Davin.

She reached out her free hand to him with a prayer of thanksgiving in her heart.

"He's going to be all right."

Grant pulled her in tight, nestling her head against his chest. She closed her eyes and soon fell back asleep. When she awoke the next time, he was leaving, and light was seeping in the windows.

"I have to go to work," he said. "But I'll come by later."

"Thank you, Grant." The words were so small for what she owed him and what she felt for him. Her heart was bursting with a combination of pride, longing, admiration and tenderness.

And she knew there wasn't another man in the world who could ever make her feel that way.

DAVIN AWOKE FEELING REALLY TIRED, and wondered if he was late for school. It was quiet, but everything was so bright.

Then he remembered they weren't home. They were in the mountains. But why was he sleeping in a real bed?

Aunt Amalie was sitting beside him; she seemed to be dozing. There was a window just past her. In the other direction he saw a hallway through the open door.

"Where am I?" He tried to prop himself up, and that was when he noticed his bandaged arm. He lifted it a few inches. Ow! Then let it drop back on his chest. "What happened?"

"Davin." His aunt's eyes popped open. "You're awake."

She sounded really glad about that for some reason. He felt her cool hand on his forehead, followed by a kiss.

"You're in the hospital, Davin, but everything's okay."

"A hospital?"

"Yes. In Revelstoke. Breakfast is here. Are you hungry?"

There was a tray that swiveled over his bed. His aunt removed a metal cover and he looked at soggy toast, with little packages of jam beside it. On a plastic plate sat a sectioned grapefruit, and next to it a small glass half filled with milk.

He wrinkled his nose. "I don't think so."

Amalie dug into the pocket of her coat and pulled out his favorite brand of granola bar.

"How about this? And I can get you a cold juice from the vending machine."

"Yes, please." He used his good hand to accept the granola bar. Noticing his aunt about to leave, he stopped her with another question.

"How did I end up here?"

"You don't remember?"

He shook his head, then paused, thinking, thinking...

In a flood it came back. The carton of cream. Amalie talking about how horrible his birth had been. Running away. Getting a ride from that weird guy with a beard. Then skiing...

"I think I was in an avalanche."

"So you *do* remember."

"A little. I heard you call my name. I was just raising my ski pole to let you know I'd heard, when something hit me from behind."

"That was the snow."

"Aunty, it felt like a truck—it really did. But I knew what was happening, because Grant had told me it would be hard like that. There wasn't time to do anything, but I kept my hand up, remembering what Grant said about having something stick up out of the snow."

"What a clever kid." She was stroking his forehead again, the way she did when he was sick. "That was what saved you, you know. I saw the top of your pole. It was a lucky break since you weren't wearing your transceiver."

Knowing that Grant would never have made a mistake like that, Davin hung his head. But he'd been in a hurry, and not really thinking straight. "I'm sorry. I guess I thought there wasn't any danger. After all, I skied that route with Mrs. Eitelbach last week."

"Conditions can change rapidly on the mountains."

"Yeah."

"Don't worry, Davin. Thankfully you're okay. That's what matters."

He was relieved she wasn't mad. But then, she rarely was. "How did you get me out of the snow? Did Grant have a shovel?"

"He sure did." She described what had happened when she saw his ski pole, how quickly the rest of the rescue team arrived and how everyone had worked together. When she got to the part about the helicopter ambulance, he could hardly stand it.

"I can't believe I missed the whole thing!"

His aunt gave him a funny look. "I would have been happy to."

He felt bad then, for all the worry he'd caused. He could see those lines in her forehead and knew they were there because of him.

"I'm real sorry."

"I know, honey. I'm just so grateful all you suffered was a broken arm."

He looked down at the weight that pressed on his chest. "This is so sweet. I've never had a cast before."

His aunt raised her eyebrows and gave him that funny look again. "I'll go get your juice."

IN THE HALLWAY, Amalie saw a woman walking toward her, wearing a familiar black-and-pink anorak. Of course it would have to be Denise Carter. Today of all days.

"Amalie." Denise ran fingers through hair that didn't seem to have been brushed yet this morning. "Can I speak with you?"

Amalie didn't like to bear a grudge, but right now she was definitely not up to more abuse. "I've—"

"I heard about Davin. I'm so sorry, I won't keep you but a moment."

On the woman's outstretched hand, Amalie saw the sparkle of her wedding ring. And relented. "What is it, Denise?"

"Grant stopped by this morning on his way to work. He saw my light was on…I haven't been able to sleep much this past while."

Not to feel sorry for her was impossible. Her face so clearly showed her suffering. Amalie was glad Grant had made time to talk to her. "So he told you about Helena?"

"About the pregnancy and that she may have been considering terminating? Yes. I guess we'll never know for sure if that was why Ramsey took her out to the mountains, but in my heart, I feel it's the most reasonable explanation."

"So do I." Amalie impulsively reached for the

other woman's hand. "From all accounts your husband loved you, Denise."

"I know. And I loved him." Fresh pain outlined new lines on the widow's face now. But at least this grief was pure, and would ease in time.

"I've got to apologize for the awful things I've said about you and your sister. I know there's no excuse, but I *am* sorry. I just couldn't rest until I told you that."

"I understand, Denise. Please don't worry. We've all endured enough as it is."

"THANK YOU, GRANT!" Davin looked with delight at the trading cards his hero had brought with him to the hospital.

Amalie smiled her own thanks, her heart expanding at the sight of Grant's familiar face.

"That was quite an escapade, buddy." Grant brushed the top of Davin's head with one hand, then bent to kiss Amalie lightly.

Davin seemed to approve of both gestures. He patted the bed and urged Grant to sit next to him. "Aunt Amalie says I'm to apologize for causing all that trouble, and I *am* sorry. You trained me better and I know I shouldn't have been skiing alone, without telling anyone where I was, not even carrying my transceiver."

"Buddy, you broke all the rules that night. I guess you must have been awfully upset."

Davin nodded. "Yeah, I was." He glanced at Amalie. "But I still knew better."

"I've never been so worried." Amalie couldn't stop from stroking a finger down her son's face.

"Aunty told me about the rescue...." Davin's body language perked up a little. "It sounded so sweet. I can't believe I missed all the excitement— the shoveling, and the mouth-to-mouth, and then the ambulance flying in and everything."

"Exciting it was, all right." The smile Grant shared with her had more than a touch of dry humor. "That was good thinking to thrust your ski pole up when the avalanche hit."

Davin beamed. "It happened so fast, like a wall falling from behind."

"Well, that pole definitely saved your life."

"And I remembered to keep my mouth shut," Davin said. "Plus not to panic. I was pretty scared, though."

Amalie just had to hug him. "We all were, Davin. But we kept our heads on straight. We didn't let that old mountain push us around."

She saw Grant look at her strangely. Then he, too, put his arm around Davin. And it was really nice. As if the three of them were a family.

Amalie thought of the house she'd always wanted to buy in Bloor West Village. As a dream, it didn't seem as enthralling as it once had. Could it be that *this* was what she'd truly longed for?

DAVIN WASN'T RELEASED until the following afternoon. By then he had most of the hospital staff's signatures, plus Heidi's and Matthew's, on his cast. The landlady had stopped by with a batch of fresh cookies, and Matthew had let them know he was returning to Seattle.

"I'll contact you when I get the memorial service organized," he said.

"We'll be there," Amalie promised.

A good many of the Avalanche Control workers had also come to visit Davin, and all proudly left their autographs on the cast for Davin to remember them by.

As if there was any chance he would ever forget. Although he'd learned some important lessons that night on the mountain, Davin still viewed the whole affair as an exciting adventure, and couldn't wait until his arm had healed enough that he could go out skiing again.

The resilience of the young, Amalie thought, knowing the experience would have traumatized her forever. Or would it?

She'd felt no greater terror than those minutes after the avalanche had struck, burying Davin instantly. But there'd been something magical about that rescue. Watching, helping, people working together, losing personal egos completely in the desire to save a life.

"We aren't going back to Toronto yet, are we?" Davin had asked anxiously.

Amalie wasn't sure how to answer that. They'd stay until the memorial service in Seattle, of course. It wouldn't make sense to drive all the way back to Toronto, then travel across Canada again, to go to the service.

But Matthew would have the service organized within the week. What would happen after?

Davin chattered the whole drive back to the apartment building. Grant was at work, but he'd promised to come by later, for dinner. Amalie was planning to impress both him and Davin with her spinach and cottage cheese manicotti. All in all, she felt she had several things to smile about as she turned down the familiar street.

Only to find a vehicle parked in her usual spot. A plain white van. Something about it made her frown, but then Heidi waving from the front door distracted her.

"Come in already!" the Swiss lady was calling. "I've made hot chocolate."

CHAPTER EIGHTEEN

BY THE TIME Amalie dragged Davin away from Heidi's minifeast, it was already two in the afternoon. She insisted he lie down for a nap while she began the preparations for dinner.

Once the manicotti were stuffed and the tomato sauce was simmering, Amalie picked up the phone to call her parents.

"Amalie? Finally. We hadn't heard from you in so long we were starting to worry."

"Well, we did have a bit of a disaster here. Or a near disaster, at any rate."

"A disaster? Just a minute...Fred? Pick up the phone in the bedroom. Amalie's on the line."

Seconds later, her father's muted voice traveled over the line. "You there, Amalie?"

"Yes, Dad. How's your back?"

"The specialist couldn't find anything wrong. Guess I'm just going to have to put up with the pain. What was this about a disaster?"

Amalie told them about Matthew Stanway's visit, his unexpected news.

"Helena was pregnant? Not really a disaster, is it? At least she was married this time."

"If she'd lived, it might have been. Have you forgotten what the doctors said after Davin was born?" Apparently, they had. There was no reply, so Amalie took a deep breath and then explained about Davin's accident and subsequent rescue in the mountains.

"Bottom line is he had a big scare—we all did. He's okay, though. His arm is broken, but it won't take long to heal."

"I can't believe he would run off like that," her mother said. "You raised him better."

"Oh, Mom." Couldn't she just be glad he was all right?

"When are you coming home?" her father asked. "I was thinking of making an appointment with a chiropractor in Toronto, but wanted to make sure you'd be able to drive me this time."

Amalie stared at the receiver, wondering what it would take to turn their focus to Davin's well-being, rather than their own.

She'd always thought they *felt* things, just didn't put their feelings to words. Now she could no longer believe that. They truly hadn't cared about Helena. And they didn't care about Davin, either. Anger made her bold.

"I don't know, Dad. I'm actually considering moving here. I've met a very nice man."

"A man?" Her mother's voice was shrill. "But you've only been gone a few weeks."

"His name's Grant Thorlow and he heads the Avalanche Control Center at Rogers Pass."

"Has he asked you to marry him?"

"No," she had to admit, "he hasn't."

"Does he know about Davin?"

"Of course he knows about Davin." Amalie couldn't keep the irritation out of her voice any longer. "He dug him out of the avalanche, saved his life. For your information, Grant is very fond of Davin, Mother."

"Maybe now. But when he sees the day-to-day responsibility of raising a child…"

"Oh, Mom. Couldn't you just be happy for me?" Of course not, she suddenly realized. Because they didn't care about her, either. Not really. Oh, as long as she went along with what they said, they were fine. But any time she tried to do something just for herself, there they were, urging her back inside the line.

"I have to go Mom, Dad. I'll call you later in the week, once I've made up my mind for sure."

She hung up on their protests, then sank into a chair.

What had she just done? Told her parents she was moving to Revelstoke when she herself hadn't even decided. But wasn't it what she wanted? So what if Grant hadn't asked her to marry him. Maybe he didn't feel he knew her well enough yet.

But she knew him well enough. In fact, she felt as though she'd known him forever.

Love. She'd had no idea it would be this wonderful—

A sound from Davin's bedroom sent her running to his room. She found him sleeping, his hair a pale halo on the stark white pillowcase. On the floor was a book. It must have slid off his sleeping bag.

Amalie stroked his cheek. His eyes immediately flew open.

"I'm sorry. Did I wake you?"

He propped himself up on his good arm. "No. I was just lying here, listening to you on the phone. Are we really going to move to Revelstoke?"

She brushed back a strand of his hair. "Would you like that?"

"Oh, yeah!" He paused for a moment. "I *would* kind of miss Jeremy, though."

Amalie nodded. And she would miss Jenny. The breath of sanity in her crazy-busy world. But Jenny had her own husband, her own family, and Amalie wanted a chance for the same. "Maybe we should think about it, right?"

"I guess."

"That's my boy." She ruffled his hair, thinking she really had to remember to be more careful in the future. The walls in this building…what else had Davin overheard?

"You know, Davin, your mother had a hard time delivering you when you were born. But no one blames babies for hard deliveries. It's not their fault."

He thought about that for a while. "You keep calling her my mother, but I don't think of her that way."

"Oh?"

"She never cared about me. She never visited me. There isn't one picture of me in this place. Or of you or Grandma or Grandpa. I don't think she loved any of us."

Amalie had been so busy she'd almost forgotten. "Wait a second, Davin. I want to show you something."

She went into her room, to the bag of Helena's personal effects she'd picked up at the hospital.

Autopsy results had confirmed Helena's pregnancy at just over thirteen weeks. So there'd been no abortion—which gave credence to the theory that Ramsey had taken her to the mountain so she could make that decision.

Now Amalie sorted through the clothing Helena had been wearing that day, for the bag containing the jewelry that had been on her person.

The small plastic packet contained a gold Piaget

watch, diamond stud earrings, a long gold chain with a locket...

Amalie took the chain and locket back to Davin's room and sat on the floor next to his sleeping bag. "See this? Your mo—I mean, Helena, was wearing this when she died."

A jab from the end of her thumbnail released the catch, and the locket separated, revealing two pictures. The first was of a white-blond-haired woman with blue eyes.

"Was that her?" Davin asked.

"No. See that pink dress? I saved my baby-sitting money for six months to buy that for my high-school graduation." Helena, of course, had never graduated. She'd been working and living on her own already. Maybe, Amalie mused, her sister had just figured out their parents a lot quicker than she had.

She shifted her finger so Davin could see the picture on the opposite side of the locket. It was a miniature of a tiny, red-skinned baby.

"That was you when you were born." Amalie handed him the locket. "Helena had her faults, Davin, I know that's true. But she loved us both."

Maybe more than they'd ever guessed. Was it possible Helena, too, had feared that seeing Davin would make her regret her decision to give him up? Was that why she'd never visited?

Davin took the locket, smudged his finger over

the pictures, then buffed them clean with the corner of his sleeping bag. Amalie saw tears gathering in his eyes, and longed to hold him close.

Tentatively, she touched his shoulder. "I know she loved you, Davin, and even though you don't feel it, she *is* your real mother."

Davin's shoulder trembled slightly. She pulled him closer. "But in my heart I can't believe she loved you more than I do. I can't believe anyone could. From the moment you were born, I thought you were the most perfect child in the world, and I still do."

"Oh, Mom!" Davin's good arm shot up around her neck, and a sob shuddered through his body.

"Oh, my baby." Amalie cradled him close, that word still ringing in her ears, the most beautiful word in the entire world.

Mom.

DAVIN FELL ASLEEP for real around five o'clock. Amalie was aware of the setting sun as she placed napkins around the table and prepared a salad. It would be a long time before the disappearance of daylight didn't remind her of those minutes of terror on that mountain.

Minutes of terror that could have ended tragically, but hadn't.

Amalie had dozens of vivid memories of Grant from that night. His tall, powerful body in front of her on the ski trail. His expression of dread when the avalanche released. The ruthless determination while he was shoveling, then his fast action in applying CPR.

Finally, and most moving for her, his tenderness when covering Davin on the stretcher.

Every step of the way he'd shown control and competence, leaving no doubt that he knew how to handle the emergency. Yet, at the same time, how much he cared had been obvious.

Now she thought again about his invitation the night they'd made love. Not to marry him, no, but to stay, and that was something.

As the hour for him to arrive approached, Amalie's stomach grew tighter and tighter. Anticipation, hope, fear…

Would he have changed his mind? Since the bodies had been recovered, there was no reason for her and Davin to delay their departure past the date of the memorial service. Would he ask her once more to stay?

If he did, Amalie had decided she would say yes.

True, asking her to move to Revelstoke did not constitute a proposal. Maybe she *was* crazy, to consider uprooting her life for a man who might *never* marry her. After all, they'd never even discussed the possibility.

But Amalie knew this was the one time she had

to do something, not because it was practical but because it was what she wanted. Needed.

Amalie glanced at the clock on the stove, the watch on her wrist. *Oh, please, let it be six soon!*

With time on her hands, she changed her sweater, put on perfume, a touch of makeup. After a momentary pause, she slipped Helena's locket over her head. Her sister's more expensive jewelry was not her style. She'd already returned most of it to Matthew and would take the watch and earrings with her when she drove out for the memorial service.

But this locket would help her hold Helena to her heart. As soon as possible, Amalie intended to replace the photo of herself with one of her sister.

A knock at the door startled, then delighted, her. Somehow Grant had bypassed the security downstairs. And arrived twenty minutes early to boot!

She rushed to the door and opened it in a wide arc.

Then froze as a tall, slim man placed a hand on the door frame, preventing her from shutting him out.

"It's been six weeks, Helena. And I'm getting tired of waiting for your answer."

GRANT INSPECTED HIS NEW HAIRCUT in the window of Flowers from the Heart. It had never occurred to him that buying roses in Revelstoke on February 14 might be difficult.

"You really should have placed an order in advance for Valentine's Day." The young girl behind the counter had short blond hair, spiked with gel and glittering with metallic sparkles. He didn't think she was old enough to understand how important this was to him.

"You mean to tell me you don't have any roses? None at all?" He stared at a beautiful long-stemmed arrangement in the glassed-in refrigerated area.

The clerk followed his gaze and shrugged. "Those were ordered two weeks ago. We do have some *pink* roses left." She nodded to a vase, which contained five tiny buds.

For a moment he considered. Then shook his head. No. He was trying to make a statement here. And that statement required a dozen long-stemmed roses.

As he considered his options, he heard bells from the door behind him. He turned and saw a man in a suit and trench coat stomping snow from his boots. Grant glanced away, then quickly back.

What do you want to bet this is the guy...

Sure enough, the man leaned over the counter and pointed to the beautiful arrangement of red roses. Willingly, the clerk pulled them out and set them on the counter.

She glared in Grant's direction, then turned to her customer. "Yes, Mr. Elliott, we have your flowers. Let me wrap them up in plastic for you so they don't get shocked by the cold.''

Grant sidled nearer to the man. ''For your wife?'' he asked, tilting his head at the bouquet the clerk was now fussing over.

The man nodded.

''Been married long?''

''Fifteen years,'' the man said, keeping his eyes on the flowers.

''So things are obviously pretty secure. You aren't having problems with your relationship or anything?''

''Now, look here.'' The man faced him. ''Do we know each other?''

Grant held his arms up apologetically. ''Sorry. I didn't mean to get personal. It's just—I'm planning to ask a woman to marry me tonight. I have no idea if she'll say yes. In fact, I think the cards are kind of stacked against me. What would you say...''

The man shifted his body back a few inches. ''Hey, you seem like a nice guy. But my wife really likes roses.''

The clerk returned with the flowers. Carefully, she placed them in the suited man's hands. She glowered at Grant. ''You'd better stop harassing the customers or I'm going to have to ask you to leave.''

''Is that right?'' Getting thrown out of a florist shop made for an amusing picture, but the situation wasn't all that funny. He stared at the cellophane package in the other man's hands. He just *had* to get those flowers....

AMALIE RECOGNIZED HER CALLER as the man who'd been watching her at the Rock Slide Saloon after her dance with Grant. She couldn't think of any legitimate reason for him to want to speak with her. Panicked, she drew back the door, intending to slam it on his fingers. But he anticipated the move and used his shoulder to wedge the door open.

"Please don't burn me off, Helena. If you've decided the answer is no, don't I at least deserve an explanation?"

He didn't sound dangerous. Amalie decided he didn't look dangerous, either. Just tired, and maybe even a little distraught. After a glance at Davin's closed bedroom door, she stepped out into the hall to clear up the mistake.

"I'm sorry to tell you this, but I'm not Helena. She died in an avalanche about three weeks ago. I'm her twin sister, Amalie."

"Come on!" Disbelief widened her unexpected visitor's blue eyes. "Helena, I know you have your reservations about bringing me back into Davin's life, but you don't need to lie—"

"Davin?" The floor under her feet seemed suddenly unstable. "What is your name?"

The man stepped back, shaken by the intensity

of her tone. "You know very well..." His gaze zoomed in on her, and he drew a quick breath. "You're not Helena. You *are* her twin."

He took another step back, his shoulders slumping, hands dropping to his side. "Did Helena really die?"

He appeared shattered by the possibility. Amalie hated to confirm it. "I'm afraid she did."

"Oh, God, this is so unfair!" He turned to the wall and hit his forehead against it.

Amalie was remembering one of her rare visits to Toronto to visit Helena after she'd moved out. Helena had thrown a small party to introduce her to her new friends.

"You're Davin's father, aren't you?"

CHAPTER NINETEEN

GRANT WAS WHISTLING the same tune that had been plaguing him for weeks, as he drove down the freshly plowed road leading to Amalie's apartment. On the passenger seat next to him sat a bottle of champagne and the dozen long-stemmed roses.

He'd offered the man at the florist's a private, guided tour into the backcountry for him and his wife and a couple of their friends in exchange for the flowers. He sure hoped the man's wife liked skiing. He'd hate to see fifteen years of marriage jeopardized.

Still, it was for a good cause.

He wasn't sure what his chances were of talking Amalie into staying, but the way she'd looked at him in the hospital gave him hope.

Good, here at last. Grant pulled to the side of the road, jogged up the sidewalk to the front security door. He sang a few more bars, frowned as a missing phrase tugged at his memory, then twirled on the spot, remembering Amalie in his arms while this very song was playing at the Rock Slide Saloon.

If he had to put his finger on the moment he'd fallen in love with her, that would be it. No wonder he couldn't get the damn tune out of his mind!

He jabbed the button beside Helen Fremont's name.

But it was Amalie he wanted to see. Amalie…

Finally she buzzed him up. He took the stairs two at a time, cradling the roses in one arm, like a baby, hanging on to the bottle of champagne with the other. Surprisingly, the door was ajar. With no hand free to knock, he nudged it open, and immediately saw Amalie sitting on the sofa, her expression blank, her posture limp.

Fear hit him like a wall of avalanching snow from behind. Something bad had happened. Or else she was planning to break off their relationship.

"What is it, Amalie? What's wrong?" He set his gifts on the floor and went to her. Sat next to her on the sofa and put his arm over her shoulders.

Her sigh might have been the air deflating from his hopes.

"Is Davin okay?"

"He's fine. Sleeping in his room."

That was a relief. "Then what…?"

"I've just had the most unexpected visitor. I still can't believe it."

Grant's mind stalled, trying to guess. "Tell me."

Amalie finally turned to face him. He could see she'd been crying. "It was Davin's father, Grant.

His name is Bobby Bradshaw, and he works for the
Pizza Paradise franchise.''

"How do you know he's Davin's father? And
why is he showing up now, of all times?''

"I'd met Helena's boyfriend once, but it was
many years ago and for a very brief time. I didn't
recognize him at first. But when he told me his
story, it all made sense.''

Grant shifted on the couch, drawing Amalie
closer.

"Bobby was in the Rock Slide Saloon that day
Ralph Carlson brought Helena in for a drink.''

"When she first arrived in town?''

"Right. He waited until she went to use the
washroom, then stopped her to talk. He told her
he'd always regretted walking away from his child
and asked for the chance to meet him.''

"Just meet him?''

"As a starting point. Bobby said he was willing
to let Davin decide, after that, whether he wanted
to continue to spend time with him.''

Grant brushed a hand over his unusually stiff
hair. "Man-oh-man...'' He remembered Amalie
saying that one of her regrets over Helena's death
was that Davin would never know who his father
was. So this was a good thing. But the timing; man,
the timing really sucked.

"That's why Helena decided to stay in Revelstoke,'' Amalie continued. "Not because of her

tires, but because she wanted to think over Bobby's request. He passes through town about once every three weeks. She was supposed to give him an answer about whether she'd let him see Davin, only she kept putting him off.''

"Until it was too late."

"Yes." Amalie pressed her cheek against his chest. "Bobby saw me dancing with you at the Rock Slide and couldn't understand why I was ignoring him. He thought I was Helena."

"Amalie, this is incredible. What are you going to do?"

She twisted her face up so she could see him. He liked having her curled beside him like this. The fear he'd suffered earlier was fading. This wasn't the end of the world. They could handle this. Whatever she decided, he would support her.

"I think we should let him talk to Davin. What do you think?"

Grant's heart and hopes swelled at the way she included him in the equation. "To tell you the truth, I'm feeling a touch of jealousy. Lately, I've been seeing myself in the role of Davin's dad."

Nervously, he checked her expression. Good. She was smiling. It was sort of misty, true, but it was a smile.

"Still," he said, "I agree Davin should have the chance to meet his biological father."

Amalie threw both arms tightly around his neck.

He buried his face against her hair, so glad to feel her in his arms again. After a few minutes, he pulled back.

"Could I check on Davin?"

She nodded, the same teary smile returning to her face. "I just wanted him to take a nap, but I think he's out for the night."

AMALIE LEANED BACK on the sofa and put her hands to her stomach. The nerves that had twisted her insides like malleable bread dough had finally subsided. Bobby Bradshaw showing up out of the blue like that had been a shock, but everything would be all right. Grant's reaction had totally reassured her. Nothing he could've said would have made her feel better.

She'd phone Bobby later, at his motel, after she'd talked to Davin in the morning. She had no idea how Davin would react to the prospect of meeting his father. But she had a hunch that whatever Bobby's role in Davin's life turned out to be, Grant would be the number one man he would look up to.

Feeling better, stronger, she stood and stretched. On her first deep breath, she noticed an odor—

Oh, Lord, it was her dinner. She'd put it in the oven before Bobby came to the door, then had forgotten all about it.

Amalie rushed to the oven and checked the casserole. The top was almost black, the edges dried and shriveled. She was staring at the charred remains when Grant came up beside her. In his hands, he held a bunch of flowers and a slender green bottle.

"Dinner?" He peered into the glass dish in her hands.

"Manicotti." She sighed. "My specialty."

"Hmm. Must be a *very* old family recipe."

She set it down on the counter and turned off the oven. He passed her the long-stemmed flowers.

"Did you know it was Valentine's Day?" he asked.

"I'd completely forgotten." The flowers were beautiful. Perfect. She hated to put them in a plastic jug, but Helena hadn't owned a vase. The flowers looked lovely anyway.

"Thank you, Grant." She turned toward him, and his arms came around her. Her gaze fell on the green bottle he'd set on the counter. "Champagne, too?"

He reached a finger under her chin. "In case you haven't noticed, I was planning to woo you tonight."

She looked at the dehydrated casserole on the counter. "Me, too," she admitted.

"Trying to convince me to move back to Toronto with you?" Now his hands were cupping her face. His expression was totally serious. "Because I will.

Maybe not to the city, but someplace north. I'd have to pull some strings with Parks Canada.''

She thought of that dance they'd had in the bar, how perfectly their bodies had fit and swayed, as if they both interpreted the music in exactly the same way.

"Never. Wrong habitat. You belong here. In these mountains.''

"But your parents—''

"Are going to have to learn to look after themselves. Grant, they've never really accepted Davin in the family. They didn't care enough about Helena to come down when you found the bodies. They won't even come to the memorial service in Seattle. After talking to them today, I don't think they even care about my happiness.''

She began to run her fingers through his hair, then paused. "You had your hair cut. *Professionally.*''

"This morning. I figured I needed all the help I could get. After Davin's accident you must be more scared of this place than ever—''

She put a finger to his mouth. "Actually, no. It's the strangest thing… I think it was watching the Avalanche Control team at work, and *you*, maybe even a little of my own reaction, too.''

"What are you saying?''

"I don't have that same fear. Avalanches are a force beyond human control, I know, and yet the things we do—the things *you* do—can have an influence. If you're properly trained, prepared and show the mountains the respect they deserve.''

''Yes.'' He held her hand in both of his. ''You get it.''

''I wonder how many lives you've saved already.'' She looked him full in the eyes, and knew she'd never get the answer from him.

''And how many you have yet to save. I don't want to take you away from here, Grant. I realized on the mountain it's part of the reason I love you.''

''Thank you.'' He kissed her then. A kiss that promised safety and security, as well as that hint of adventure that would always be part of their lives.

''I love you, Amalie. And I really want to marry you. I don't know if you're ready to believe this, but you're one of the bravest women I've ever met.''

''Don't forget beautiful.'' She kissed his chin. ''And sexy.'' Then slid her lips down the column of his neck.

''Yes, and yes.'' He ran his hands down her back, cupped her buttocks and groaned. ''Amalie, it looked to me that Davin was sleeping really *soundly*.''

''Is that so?'' Amalie brought her mouth back to within inches of his. She felt him growing hard against her. ''I guess I won't bother with dinner, then.''

"I love a woman with a good set of priorities."
He picked her up easily and carried her down the
hall.

A blast of air set the windowpanes on the west
side of the apartment to rattling. A new storm front
was moving into the Rogers Pass. Eight inches of
snow were expected to fall on the Selkirks before
sunrise. The highway would have to be closed,
more avalanche control work undertaken.

But for Amalie and Grant, wrapped in the
warmth of an old quilt and their newfound love, the
snow and the cold were irrelevant. Their forecast
was for clear skies and very hot temperatures. And
a lifetime together.

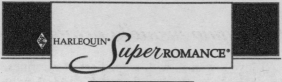

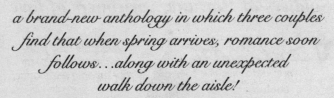

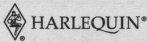